CRITICAL ACCLAIM FOR
LAWRENCE BLOCK

"Block is one of the best!"　　　　　—*Washington Post*

"Block's fiction is tense and energetic. His stories unfold smoothly and elegantly, with plenty of detail and rich characterization."　　　　　—*Houston Chronicle*

"Block's style is utterly telling in every line."
　　　　　—*Publishers Weekly*

"Larry Block has always been at least three steps ahead of most writers in originality and readability."
　　　　　—*Harlan Ellison*

ALSO BY LAWRENCE BLOCK
Published by ibooks, inc.:

After the First Death
You Could Call It Murder
Deadly Honeymoon
Such Men Are Dangerous

ABOUT THE AUTHOR

LAWRENCE BLOCK's novels range from the urban noir of Matthew Scudder (*Hope to Die*) to the urbane effervescence of Bernie Rhodenbarr (*The Burglar in the Rye*), while other characters include the globetrotting insomniac Evan Tanner (*Tanner On Ice*) and the introspective assassin Keller (*Hit List*). He has published articles and short fiction in *American Heritage, Redbook, Playboy, GQ,* and *The New York Times,* and has published several collections of short fiction in book form, the most recent being his *Collected Mystery Stories.* Block is a Grand Master of Mystery Writers of America. He has won the Edgar and Shamus awards four times and the Japanese Maltese Falcon award twice, as well as the Nero Wolfe award. In France, he has been proclaimed a Grand Maitre du Roman Noir and has twice been awarded the Societe 813 trophy. He has been a guest of honor at Bouchercon and at book fairs and mystery festivals in France, Australia, Italy, New Zealand and Spain, and, as if that were not enough, was presented with the key to the city of Muncie, Indiana. He is a past president of the Private Eye Writers of America and the Mystery Writers of America.

COWARD'S
KISS

LAWRENCE BLOCK

ibooks
new york
www.ibooks.net

DISTRIBUTED BY SIMON & SCHUSTER, INC.

A Publication of ibooks, inc.

© U.S. Edition 2003 Lawrence Block

First published by Fawcett Gold
Medal Books in 1961 under the title
Death Pulls a Doublecross. A 1987
edition with the title *Coward's Kiss*
was published by the Countryman
Press, Woostock, Vermont.

An ibooks, inc. Book

Distributed by Simon & Schuster, Inc.
1230 Avenue of the Americas, New York, NY 10020

ibooks, inc.
24 West 25th Street
New York, NY 10010

The ibooks World Wide Web Site Address is:
http://www.ibooks.net

ISBN 0-7434-5899-0
First ibooks, inc. printing June 2003
10 9 8 7 6 5 4 3 2 1

Cover design by Mike Rivilis

Printed in the U.S.A.

ONE

IT was the right kind of night for it.

The afternoon had been tattletale gray that slowly turned to black. It had been warm and it got warmer, with humidity hanging in the air like crepe. All afternoon New York had crouched under a dark sky and waited for the rain to come.

I ate a quick and tasteless supper at the delicatessen around the corner, then went back to my apartment and stacked records on the hi-fi. I sat in a chair by the window, smoking a pipe and listening to the music and watching the night roll in like smoky fog.

It was a dark night, a coat of flat black paint that masked the moon and stars. Somewhere between eleven and twelve it started to rain. By that time the winds were ready. They came in behind the rain and brought it down hard and fast. I took Mozart off the hi-fi and put on a Bartók quartet—the slashing dissonance matched the mood of the turbulent weather outside. It was the kind of night nice people stayed safe and sound in their own apartments, stared at television sets and went to sleep early.

I hoped all the nice people who lived on East Fifty-first Street would do just that.

When the record ended I turned off the hi-fi and went to the closet. I put on the trench coat and slouch hat that every good private detective picks up the day he gets his license. Then I rolled up the oriental rug in the front hall and took it out of the apartment with me. I walked down a flight of stairs and out of my brownstone into the rain.

The weather was even worse than I had thought.

5

Drops of water bounced off my trench coat. Others rolled off the hat. Still others found their way into the bowl of my pipe and put it out for me. I stuffed my pipe into a pocket and started walking. I had the rug under my arm like a king-size pumpernickel.

I keep my car in a garage around the corner on Third between Eighty-fourth and Eighty-fifth. The kid on duty there has a bad case of acne, plus some adenoids that get in his way when he tries to talk.

"Mr. London," he said. "You want your car on a night like this?"

I told him I did. He put down a Batman comic and ran off to find it while I brushed raindrops off the roll of rug. He brought the Chevy around and presented me with the keys with what was supposed to be a flourish.

"You better keep the top up," he said. "Convertible's not much fun in this kind of rain. Man, you put the top down and you'll drown in there."

I gave him a quarter and hoped he'd put it toward an operation. I dropped the rug in the back seat and got behind the wheel. I glanced over at the kid to see whether he was busy wondering where the hell I was carrying a rug at twelve-thirty in the morning. He didn't seem to care. His nose was buried in the comic book and he was off in a private world inhabited by Batman, Robin and the Joker. I started the car and drove away feeling more like the Joker than Batman.

I took Second Avenue downtown and headed for Fifty-first Street—the address Jack Enright had given me—111 East Fifty-first Street. The address was impressive. I guess if you're going to keep a mistress you might as well do it in style. Jack's mistress was a blonde named Sheila Kane and I was on my way to meet her.

Traffic was light on Second Avenue. A handful of cabs cruised slowly, waiting to be hailed by the drinkers and drunks who use the avenue's cocktail lounges as a home away from home. There were very few pedestrians. New York stays awake twenty-four hours a day, even in the middle of the week, but that only holds for a few sections of the city. Times Square, bits of Greenwich Village, parts of Harlem. The residential neighborhoods go to bed early.

Fifty-first Street was already going to bed. A few hours later all the lights would be out and all eyes would be closed. When everyone's asleep, a single walking man is cause for suspicion. This was the best time to pass unnoticed.

I drove past number 111 slowly. There was no doorman; no flunkey on duty. I circled the block and found a parking space two doors east of the building. I got out of the Chevy and left it there, lugging the carpet roll to the building's doorway.

I stood for a moment or two in the vestibule, studying the names of the tenants. Three others shared the fourth floor with Miss S. Kane. There was a P.D. Huber, an Angela Weeks, a Mrs. Aaron Clyman. I hoped they were all sleeping peacefully. I wasn't worried about Sheila Kane. It was a hell of an hour to pay a call on her, but I knew she couldn't care less.

She was dead.

One of the keys Jack Enright had given me fit the outer door. I let myself in, carried the carpet to the elevator. It was a self-service affair and it was slower than a retarded child. I piloted it to the fourth floor, got out of it, then left my own keycase wedged between the door and the jamb. That way nobody could steal it away from me. I wanted it to be there waiting when I was ready for it.

One of the doors had a neat brass nameplate that told me Sheila Kane lived there, which wasn't eaxctly true. I stuck Jack's other key into the lock and turned it. The door opened silently. I walked inside, closed the door, then felt around for the light switch. The room was very dark. Somewhere, in another apartment, someone was listening to 'Death and Transfiguration.' It was in tune with everything else.

When I switched on the light I knew how Jack must have felt. It was quite a shock.

The living room was large and the thick gray carpeting that ran wall-to-wall made it look still larger. Well-chosen pieces of French Provincial furniture rimmed the

7

room and left a large oval of carpetted floor in the middle. In the precise center of the oval was the girl.

She wore stockings and a garter belt and nothing else and she looked nuder than nude. The full effect was surrealistic, a grisly joke by Dali in three dimensions. The room itself was too neat to be true. Nothing was out of place. There were no ashes in the ashtrays, no empty glasses on the table tops. There was just a girl, flat on her back, arms outstretched, almost nude, with a hole in her face. A little blood reddened the carpet near her head and matted her blonde hair.

She must have been pretty. She wasn't now, because the face is the center of beauty and there was nothing beautiful about that face now. Death was its only expression and death is not beautiful. Corpses do not look as though they are sleeping. They look dead.

Her body tried to deny that death. It was so young and rounded and firm and pink it almost looked alive. The breasts were firm, the waist slender, the legs long and lovely.

I left her and looked around the apartment. I checked the other rooms—a bedroom, a bathroom, a tiny kitchen. The neatness was almost overpowering. The bed was made, the sink scrubbed, the dishes washed and put away. I wondered why the killer had stripped her, or half-stripped her, and I wondered what he had done with her clothes. Carried them away with him, maybe. As souvenirs of death.

It didn't make much sense. When one gangster shoots down another gangster it doesn't matter a hell of a lot and the world doesn't lose by the killing. This was something else. It doesn't make sense when someone kills a pretty girl.

What I had to do was tasteless. I didn't want to do it. I wanted to go home and pretend I didn't know anybody named Jack Enright, that I had never been to a fourth-floor apartment on East Fifty-first Street. That there was no girl named Sheila Kane, that she wasn't lying dead on her living room floor.

I went back to the living room and stood looking at her for too many seconds. Then I grabbed the rug I'd brought

8

and rolled it out next to her. It was just the right size. I kneeled down next to her and rolled a-little-over-a-hundred pounds of carbon and hydrogen onto the rug. Her flesh was cold and she was heavy now, cold and heavy with death. I got her onto the rug and rolled her and the carpet together until I wound up with a package that looked like nothing more than a thick roll of carpet.

Then I went to her bathroom, her very neat and very immaculate bathroom. I lifted the lid of a spotless toilet and threw up. I felt a little better after that.

I gave the apartment a once-over before leaving it forever. While I walked around the place I had the feeling it was a waste of time, that I wouldn't find anything. I was right.

There couldn't have been anything to see there. It was a good apartment, a pleasant apartment, but I got the impression that no one could possibly have lived there. Everything was put together like a stage set. There was nothing extraneous, nothing without a purpose. A desk on stage which is never opened will have empty drawers. Sheila Kane's apartment radiated this feeling. Her personality had left no stamp on the place. The apartment stood alone, well-furnished and well-arranged, waiting for a rental agent to show it to prospective tenants. But some fool had been dumb enough to leave a corpse in the middle of the living room.

I found a throw rug in a closet and covered the bloody part of the carpet with it. That would do unless someone searched the apartment carefully, and when that happened the bloodstains would be found no matter what I did to hide them. Then I picked up the roll of rug with the girl's body in it and carried it to the doorway. It was heavier now. Too heavy.

I turned off the light again, opened the door. My key case still held the elevator for me. Somewhere somebody was ringing for it impatiently. I carried my package into it, pushed the button. The door closed and we rode slowly down to the first floor.

A woman was waiting for the elevator. A gray, fifty-ish woman with a sable stole and a lorgnette. She held a closed umbrella in one hand.

9

"That rain," she said. "Terrible."

"Is it still raining?"

She smiled at me. Everything about her told me that her husband had had the decency to die well-insured. "Just a drizzle," she said. "But these elevators. They should have a boy to run them. So slow."

I smiled back at her. She got into the elevator and rode to the third floor, which meant she probably hadn't known Sheila Kane. I left the building knowing that she wouldn't remember me. She was a woman who lived in a world of her own. That rain and that elevator were her major problems.

The rain had eased up, but the night was as dark as ever. Streetlights tried to brighten things and failed. I carried the rug through the gloom to the car. It went in the back seat. I went in the front seat and the car went to Fifth Avenue, then uptown to Central Park. Traffic was even thinner now. I checked the mirror now and then to make sure nobody was following me. Nobody was.

Central Park is an oasis in a desert or a wilderness in the middle of a jungle, depending on how you look at it. I drove through it, left the wide roads for the twisting lanes, let the Chevy follow its nose. I found a spot and pulled off onto the grass at the side of the road. I killed the engine and climbed out onto grass that was soft and wet from all that rain. The air was so fresh and clean that it didn't seem like New York at all.

That much was good. If she had to lie dead, at least she should do so in a fresh clean spot. But it was a shame about the rain. There was something very indecent about spilling her out nude and dead in the dampness. There was something. . . .

I opened the back door and picked up the rug again, and by this time I was beginning to feel like an Armenian delivery boy. I held onto one end of the rug and let it spill out. The rug unwound neatly and what was left of Sheila Kane hit the ground, rolled over twice and came to rest face down on the grass.

There was a flashlight in the Chevy's glove compartment. I got it; took a last look at the girl. The bullet hadn't lodged in her head. There was a small and neatly rounded hole in the back of her head where it had made its exit. I thought about modern police methods and scientific laboratory techniques and decided they would figure out that she had been killed by a white male between thirty and thirty-two years of age, wearing a blue pea jacket and favoring his right foot when he walked. Science is wonderful. All I could tell from the hole was that the killer had picked up the bullet from the apartment, and I'd guessed that all along.

I turned off the flashlight. I rolled up the damned rug and tossed it back in the car, feeling very sick of rugs and corpses, of the smell of Central Park and of the smell of death. I thought about Sheila Kane, shrouded in darkness in tall wet grass. I thought about Newton's law of inertia. Bodies at rest were supposed to remain at rest, but the dead girl had broken that law. She wasn't supposed to be moving around. And how long would it be before they let her rest? A quick ride to the morgue. An autopsy. And then another ride, slow and sedate, and a final home under the ground.

I got back into the Chevy, put it in low and got the hell out of Central Park. I dropped the rug at my apartment—there was no point shoving it in the garage kid's nose—and ran the car back to the garage. I turned it over to Adenoids and Pimples.

"Crazy night," he told me.

"Crazy?"

"That's where it's at." He shifted a wad of gum from one side of his mouth to the other, knocked ashes off a filter-tipped cigarette. He gave me a grin that he could have kept to himself.

"A night to get killed on," he said. "That type night."

I didn't have an answer handy.

"Spooky-kooky, what I mean. Me, I'm happy. I live right, Mr. London. I don't cut work until the sun comes up. Midnight to dawn, that's my scene. I wouldn't walk around on a night like this. I couldn't make it."

"I'm walking home."

"Take a hack," he told me. "You live far?"

"Not far."

11

"You could get hit on the head. Knifed, even. How far do you live?"

"Around the corner," I said. "I think I'll chance it."

"Ruck, anyway."

I looked at him.

"Rotsa Ruck. Like they say in China."

They don't, but I wasn't going to argue with him. I left him there and walked back to the apartment. Nobody knifed me and nobody hit me over the head, which wasn't much of a surprise. I put my rug back in the hall where it belonged and sponged a few drops of caked blood from it. There were probably traces of blood in the thing but I wasn't going to stay up nights worrying about them. Nobody would come to look at my rug. Because nobody would connect me with Sheila Kane. Because there was no connection.

Now it was time to relax, time to unwind. I found a pipe and stuffed tobacco into it. I lit it evenly all around and smoked. I poured cognac into a glass and sipped it. It was smooth and it went all the way down and left a pleasant glow in its path.

It was time to relax, but I couldn't manage it. There was a picture that stayed in my mind—a picture of a nude blonde, dead and cold, all dolled up in stockings and garter belt, with her face shot up and her hair bloody, lying in the very middle of a room that was the essence of neatness and order.

An ugly picture. A hard one to forget and a hard one to think about.

But I managed to think about something else, finally. I managed to think about my sister, whose name is Kaye. A very nice person, my sister. A lovely woman. A sweet woman.

I thought about her for a few minutes. Then I thought about her husband. His name is Jack Enright.

TWO

HE had leaned on my doorbell around three that afternoon. I had been doing the Times crossword puzzle. I stopped trying to think of a twelve-letter word for 'Son of Jocasta,' put down the paper and went to answer the door. I pushed the buzzer to unlock the downstairs door, then waited in the hallway while he worked his way up a flight of stairs. He climbed quickly and he was panting before he hit the top.

Jack Enright. My sister's husband. A tall man, forty-two or forty-three, with a reddish complexion and a little too much weight on a broad frame. A good handball player and a fair hand at squash, even though he didn't look the part. Now he didn't look the part at all.

His shoulders sagged like an antique mattress. His face was drawn, his eyes hollow. His tie was loose and his jacket was unbuttoned. He looked like hell.

He said: "I have to talk to you, Ed."

"Something the matter?"

"Everything. I have to talk to you. I'm in trouble."

I motioned him inside. He followed me into the living room like a domesticated zombie. I found a chair for him and he sat down heavily in it.

"Go ahead," I said. "What's up?"

"Ed . . ."

He said my name and let it hang there. He didn't even manage to close his mouth. I found a bottle of cognac and poured three fingers of it into an Old Fashioned glass. I gave it to him and he looked at it vacantly. I don't think he saw it.

"Drink, it Jack."

13

"It's not four o'clock," he said stupidly. "A gentleman never drinks before four o'clock. And it's———"

"It's four o'clock somewhere," I told him. "Go ahead and drink it, Jack."

He emptied the glass in a single swallow and I'm sure he never tasted it at all. Then he put down the glass and looked at me through empty eyes.

"Is something wrong with Kaye?"

"Why?"

I shrugged. "She's your wife and my sister. Why else would you come to me?"

"Kaye's fine," he said. "There's nothing wrong with Kaye."

I waited.

"I'm the one who needs some help, Ed. Badly."

"Want to tell me about it?"

He looked away. "I suppose so," he said. "I don't even know where to begin."

The drink was helping but it had its work cut out for it. It unnerved me to see a steady guy like Jack Enright that badly shaken up. He's a doctor—a very good one— a very successful one. He's got a wife who loves him and two daughters who adore him. I'd always thought of him as a strong man, a Rock-of-Gibraltar type, for my not-too-strong sister to lean on. Now he was ready to fall apart at the seams.

"Let's have it, Jack."

He said: "You've got to help me."

"I have to hear about it first."

He sighed, nodded, reached for a cigarette. His hands were shaking but he managed to get it lit. He drew a lot of smoke into his lungs and blew it out in a long thin column. I watched his eyes narrow to focus on the end of the cigarette.

"Fifty-first Street," he said. "111 East Fifty-first Street. An apartment on the fourth floor."

I waited.

"There's a girl in there, Ed. A dead girl. Somebody shot her in the . . . in the face. At close range, I think. Most of her . . . most of her face is missing. Blown off."

He shuddered.

14

"You didn't——"

"No!" His eyes screamed at me. "No, of course not. I didn't kill her. That's what you were going to ask, isn't it?"

"I suppose so. Why the hell else would you be so jumpy? You're a doctor. You've seen death before."

"Not like this."

I picked up my pipe and crammed tobacco into the bowl. I took my time lighting up while he got ready to talk some more. By the time the pipe was lit he was off again.

"I didn't kill her, Ed. I discovered the body. It was . . . a shock. Opening the door. Walking inside. Looking around, not seeing her at first. She was on the floor, Ed. How often do you look at the floor when you walk into a room. I almost . . . almost fell on her. I looked down and there she was. She was lying on her back. I looked at her and saw her and she had a hole where her face was supposed to be."

I poured more brandy into his glass. He looked at it for a second or two. Then he tossed it off.

"You called the police?"

"I couldn't."

I looked hard at him. "All right," I said evenly. "You can stumble around for the next half hour and it won't do either of us any good. Get to the point, Jack."

He looked at the rug. It's a Bokhara, a much better oriental than the length of rug in the hallway. But Jack Enright isn't especially interested in oriental rugs.

He found this one fascinating now.

"Who was she?"

"Sheila Kane."

"And——?"

"And I've been paying her rent for the past three months now," he said. He was still looking at the rug. His voice was steady, the tone slightly defiant. "I've been paying her rent, and I've been buying her clothes and I've been giving her spending money. I've been keeping her, Ed. And now she's dead."

He stopped talking. We both sat there and listened to the silence.

15

He laughed. His laughter had no humor to it. "It happens to other men," he said. "You've got a perfectly good marriage; you love your wife and she loves you. Then you listen to the song of the sirens. You meet a beautiful blonde. Why are they always blondes, Ed?"

"Sheila Kane was a blonde?"

"Sort of a dirty blonde originally. She tinted it. Her hair was all yellow-gold. She wore it long and it would cascade over her bare shoulders and—"

He stopped for another sigh. "I didn't kill her, Ed. God, I couldn't kill anybody. I'm not a killer. And I don't even own a damn gun. But I can't call the police. Christ, you know what would happen. They'd have me on the carpet for hours with the bright lights in my eyes and the questions coming over and over. They'd work me six ways and backwards. They'd rake me over the coals."

"And then they'd let you go."

"And so would Kaye." His eyes turned meek, helpless. "Your sister's a wonderful woman, Ed. I love her. I don't want to lose her."

"If you love her so much——"

"Then why did I play around? I don't know, Ed. God knows I don't make a habit of it."

"Did you love this Sheila?"

"No. Yes. Maybe . . . I don't know."

That was a big help. "How did it start?"

He hung his head. "I don't know that either. It just happened, damn it. She came to my office one day. Just wandered in off the street, picked my name out of the yellow pages. She thought she was pregnant, wanted me to examine her."

"Was she?"

"No. She'd missed a period or two and she was worried. Hell, it happens all the time. Just worrying can make a girl miss. I gave her an examination and told her she was all right. She wanted to be sure, asked me to run a test. I took a urine sample and told her I'd run it through the lab and give her a call. She said she didn't have a phone, she'd be back in two days."

"And?"

"And that was that. For the time being, anyway. The test went to the lab. It was negative, of course. She wasn't pregnant. That's what I told her when she came back."

I told him it was a funny way to start an affair.

"I suppose so," he said. He was getting steadier now, pulling himself back together again. It seemed to me that his adultery was nagging him more than the simple fact of the girl's death. Now that it was out in the open, now that he'd let his hair down in front of me, he could start to relax a little.

"She was broke, Ed. Couldn't pay me. I told her the hell with it, she could pay me when she got the chance. Or not at all. I've got a rich practice. East Side clientele. I can afford to miss out on an occasional fifteen-dollar fee. But she seemed so bothered about it that I felt sorry for her. I took her to a decent restaurant and bought her a lunch. She was a kid in a candy store, Ed. She said she'd been eating all her meals in cafeterias."

I grimaced appropriately.

"So that's how it started, Ed. Silly, isn't it? Affairs aren't supposed to start with a pelvic examination."

"They can end with one," I suggested.

He didn't laugh. "I guess I was just in the right mood for it, if you know what I mean. I was in a rut. The girls are growing up, Kaye has her women's groups, my practice is so safe and secure that it's duller than dishwater. I've got a good life and a good marriage and that's that. So I decided I was missing something. Why do men climb mountains? Because they're there. That's the way I heard it."

"And that's why you climbed Sheila Kane?"

"Just about." He lit another cigarette while I knocked the dottle out of my pipe. "I was a different person when I was with her, Ed. I was young and fresh and alive. I wasn't the old man in a rut. Hell, she had me pegged as some sort of romantic figure. I took her to a matinee or two on Broadway. I gave her books to read and records to listen to. This made me a God."

He drew on the cigarette. "It's nice, being a God. Your sister sees me as I am. That's the way a marriage

17

has to be—firm understanding, genuine acceptance, all of that. But . . . oh, the hell with it. I'm a damned fool, Ed."

"You went with her for three months. Then what happened?"

He looked at me.

"Did she start angling for marriage?"

"Oh," he said. "No, nothing like that. I was cold-blooded about it, Ed. I made up my mind that one word from her about marriage would mean it was time to walk out on her. You've got to understand that—I never stopped loving Kaye, never thought about a divorce. But Sheila was the perfect paramour, happy to sit in the shade and be there when I wanted her. It was almost terrifying, having that kind of hold over a person."

I nodded. "And now she's dead."

"Now she's dead." He made the word sound colder than dry ice.

"And you won't call the police."

"Ed . . ."

"Anonymously," I suggested. "So they can look for the killer."

He was shaking his head so hard I thought he'd lose it. "I paid her rent," he said. "I gave her checks; I spent plenty of time up at her apartment. Her neighbors would remember me and her landlord would recognize my name."

He was sweating now. He wiped sweat from his forehead with one hand. His eyes were angry and frightened at once.

"So the police will find me, Ed. They'll find me and they'll drag me in. And then they'll be sure I did it. That I killed her, that I found a gun somewhere and got rid of it somewhere. Isn't that what they'll say?"

"Probably."

"And Kaye will find out," he finished. "And you know what that will do to her."

I knew damn well what it would do to her. The marriage that seemed like a rut to Jack was Kaye's whole life. She lived in a sweet little world where the sun was always shining, where charge accounts bloomed on every

18

bush, where the worst peril was going down two doubled in an afternoon bridge session. Where her husband loved her, and loved her faithfully, and where God was in his heaven and all was right with the world.

"What do I do, Ed?"

"Let's turn that one around. What am I supposed to do for you, Jack?"

"Help me."

"How?"

He avoided my eyes. "Suppose I were a client," he said. "Suppose I came to you and——"

"I'd throw you out on your ear. Or call the cops. Or both."

"But I'm not a client. I'm you're brother-in-law."

He went on talking but I wasn't listening any more. Hell, if he was a client I had no problems. I turned him in and avoided being an accessory after the fact to murder. Because if I didn't know him, if he weren't my brother-in-law, I would have to figure him for the killer. He didn't have a gun? A hundred dollars buys you an unregistered gun in half the pawnshops in New York. On every street corner there's a sewer to toss it into when you're done with it. So he didn't have much of a case at all. A good prosecutor would tie him in Gordian knots.

"She can't be found at the apartment," I said slowly. "Or they'll connect the two of you. That's how it boils down."

He blinked, then nodded.

"Which means they can't identify her at all," I went on. "If they do, they trace her to the apartment. Then they trace her to you, all of which makes things difficult. Was she from New York?"

He shook his head.

"Know many people in town?"

"Hardly anybody. But . . ."

"Go on."

"I was just going to say that I wasn't with her all the time. She could have had some other interests. We didn't talk much about the time we spent apart."

I didn't say anything.

"I don't know, Ed. I think she was trying to get into

19

the theater. She never had a part, never talked about it. But I got the idea somewhere. She might know . . . might have known some theater people."

I said it was possible. "Still, the police would have a tough time making a positive identification. Not if she didn't wind up in her own apartment. Her fingerprints probably aren't on file anywhere. If she were found, say, in Central Park, she'd go as an unidentified victim. They might never find out her name, let alone yours. At any rate it would give you time to stall. Your checks would clear the bank and the landlord would forget your name."

"And the real killer——"

"Would go scot free," I finished for him. "Not necessarily. In the first place, you're the real killer. No, hold on—I know you didn't do it. But the police would stop looking once they hit you. They'd have enough circumstantial evidence to get an indictment without looking any farther. Meanwhile, the killer would cover his tracks."

I paused for breath. "This way they won't have you on hand as a convenient dummy. They'll have to start from scratch and they just might come up with the real killer."

He brightened visibly.

"That's not all. I'll know things they won't know. I'll be able to run my own check on Sheila Kane. Maybe somebody had a damn good reason to shoot a hole in her head. I can look around, see what I can find out."

"Do you think——"

"I don't think much of anything, to tell you the truth. I don't want your marriage to fall in. I don't want Kaye to get hurt and I don't want to see you tried for murder. So it looks as though I'll have to move a body for you."

He got up from the chair and started to pace the floor. I watched him ball one hand into a fist and smack it into the palm of the other hand. He was still a collection of loose nerves but they were starting to tighten up again.

I looked at him and tried to hate him. He married my sister and cheated on her and that ought to be cause for hatred. It didn't work out that way. You can't coin an ersatz double standard and apply it to brothers-in-law.

20

He fell on his face for a pretty blonde; hell, I'd taken a few falls for the same type of thing myself. He was married and I wasn't, but the state of matrimony doesn't alter body chemistry. He was a guy in a jam and I had to help him.

"Can I do anything, Ed?"

I shook my head. "I'll do it alone," I told him. "Not now. Later this evening when it's dark and the streets are empty. It's chancey but I'll take the chance. I'll need a key, if you've got one handy."

He fished in a pocket and came up with a set of keys. I took them from him and set them on the coffee table.

"Go on home," I said. "Try to relax."

He nodded but I don't think he heard me. "The hard part comes later," he said. "When I realize that she's really dead. Now she's part of a mess that I've gotten myself into. But in a few hours she'll turn back into a person. A person I knew well and cared a great deal about. And then it's going to be tough. I'll think about you picking her body up like a sack of flour and dumping her in the park and . . . I'm sorry. I'm going on and on like a damned fool."

I didn't say anything.

"This'll sound silly as hell, Ed. But . . . be gentle with her, will you? She was a very nice person. You would have liked her, I think."

"Jack . . ."

He brushed my hand away. "Hell with it," he said. "I'm all right. Look, give me a ring tomorrow at the office if you get the chance. And be careful."

I walked him to the door. Then I went to the front window and watched him walk a few doors down the block to his big black Buick. He sat in it for a moment, then started the motor and drove away. I looked up at the clouds and watched them get darker.

The cognac was gone. I filled the glass again and listened to words that went through my mind. 'Be gentle with her, will you?' Gentle. Roll her gently in a rug and toss her gently in a car and drop her gently in the wet grass. And leave her there.

21

It was a mess. A private detective doesn't solve a crime by suppressing evidence. He doesn't launch a murder investigation by transporting a body illegally. Instead he plays ball with the police, keeps his nose clean and collects his fees. That way he can pay too much rent for a floor-through apartment loaded with heavy furniture and Victorian charm. He can drive a convertible and smoke expensive tobacco and drink expensive cognac.

I like my apartment and my car and my tobacco and my cognac. So I make a point of playing ball with cops and keeping a clean nose.

Most of the time.

But now I had a brother-in-law instead of a client and a mess instead of a case. That shot the rule/book out the window. It gave me a dirty nose.

I looked at my watch. It was four in the morning. And at four a gentleman can drink. It's nice to be a gentleman. It puts you at peace with the world. And, although my glass was empty, there was plenty of cognac left in the bottle.

When it was empty I went to sleep.

THREE

DAWN was a gray lady with red eyes and a cigarette cough. She shook me awake by the eyelids and hauled me out of bed. I called her nasty names, stumbled into the kitchen to boil water for coffee. I washed up, brushed my teeth and shaved. I spooned instant coffee into a cup and poured boiling water over it, then lit a cigarette and tried to convince myself that I was really awake.

It was a hard selling-job. My mind was overflowing with blondes and they were all dead. There was a blonde with her face shot away, another blonde in stockings and garter belt in a surrealistic living room, a third blonde bundled snug as a corpse in a rug, a fourth blonde sprawled headlong in Central Park's wet grass.

I scalded my mouth with coffee, anesthetized it with cigarette smoke. It was time to start turning over flat rocks to find a killer and I didn't know where the rocks were. Sheila Kane was dead and I had been her undertaker, but that was all I knew about the girl. She was blonde, she was dead, she had been Jack Enright's mistress. Nothing more.

So Jack was the logical place to start. There were things I had to know and he could fill me in. I wondered how much he had left out, how much he had lied, how much he had forgotten.

And how much he had never known in the first place.

I turned the burner on under the water and dumped more instant coffee into the cup. The water boiled and I made more coffee. I was stirring it when the phone rang.

It was Jack.

23

"Did you—?"

"Everything's all right," I told him. "You can relax now. It's all taken care of."

His breath came like a tire blowing out. His words followed it just as fast. "I don't know how to thank you, Ed. You sure as hell saved my bacon. We'll have to get together. . . ."

"That's an understatement."

He hesitated and I knew why. In the Age of the Wiretap the telephone's an instrument of torture. It's like talking with an extra person in the room. I looked around for a better way to phrase things.

"I've been having trouble with my back," I said. "Been planning to drop by. Think you can fit me in sometime this afternoon?"

"Just a minute."

I waited. He came back, his tone easy, his manner professional now. "I'm all booked up but I can squeeze you in, Ed. Make it around two-thirty. Good enough?"

I looked at the clock. It was a few minutes after ten. I'd be seeing him in four and a half hours.

"Fine," I said. "I'll see you then. Take it easy, Jack."

He told me he would, mumbled something pleasant, and rang off. I stood there for a second or two with the phone in my hand, looking at the receiver and waiting for it to start talking all by itself.

Then I cradled it and went back to my coffee.

The *Times* had what story there was but you had to look hard to find it. In New York they don't stick an unidentified corpse on the front page. There are too many bodies floating around for them to do that. The tabloids might have found room for Shelia on page three or four, but the *Times* was too high-minded. They printed the full texts of speeches by Khrushchev and Castro and Adenauer and my blonde didn't even make the first section. I found her on the second page from the end under two decks of sedate eighteen-point type.

GIRL FOUND DEAD
IN CENTRAL PARK

It went on from there, straight and cold and to the point. The body of a young woman in her late teens or early twenties had been found partially nude and shot to death on the eastern edge of Central Park near 91st Street. A preliminary medical examination disclosed that the girl had not been sexually attacked and that the fatal shot had been fired at relatively close range. The slug had not been recovered, but police guessed it had come from a .32 or .38-calibre handgun. Police theorized the victim had been killed elsewhere and then transported to the park, where she was found by a night laborer on his way home from work.

There were a few more lines but they didn't have anything vital to say. I killed time thumbing through the rest of the paper, reading the world news and the national news and the local news, filling myself with vital information. Asian cholera was at epidemic strength in northern India. Reform Democrats were pushing for the overthrow of Tammany Hall. A military junta had ousted the government of El Salvador; Jersey Standard was off an eighth of a point; Telephone was up three-eighths, Polaroid down five and a half. An obscure play by Strindberg had been exhumed for presentation off-Broadway and the critics had cremated it.

At ten-thirty I folded the paper and stuck it in a wastebasket. I took a shower and got dressed. This made me officially awake, so I filled a pipe with tobacco and lit it.

And the phone rang.

I picked up the receiver and said hello to the mouthpiece. That was all I had a chance to say. the voice that bounced back at me was low and raspy. It was thick heavy New York with echoes of Brownsville or Mulberry Street beneath it.

"This London? Listen good. You got the stuff and we want it. We're not playing games."

I asked him what the hell he was talking about.

His laugh was short and unpleasant. "Play it anyway you want, London. I know where you been and what you picked up. If you got a price, fine. It's reasonable and we pay it."

"Who is this, anyway?"

No laughter this time. "Don't play hard to get, London. You got a reputation as a smart boy so be smart. You're just a private eye, smart or stupid. You're on your own. We got an organization. We can find things out and we can get things done. We know you were at the broad's apartment. We know you picked her up and dumped her. Jesus, you think you're playing tag with amateurs? We can go hard or soft, baby. You don't want to be too cute. You can get paid nice or you can get hit in the head. Anyway you want it, it's up to you."

"What do I get if I sell?"

"More than you get anywhere else." He chuckled. "We can hand you a better deal. We got——"

"An organiaztion," I said, tired of the game. "I know all about it. You told me."

He toughened up. "We hit the broad," he said, his voice grating. "We can hit you the same way. It gets messy. You might as well be smart about it."

"Go to hell."

"We'll be in touch, London. You know how they say it: Don't call us, we'll call you."

The phone clicked in my ear.

I was getting pretty damned sick of holding a dead phone in my hand. I put it down hard, stuck my pipe in my mouth. It had gone dead. I scratched a match for it and found a chair to sit in.

Things were taking their own kind of shape. I had to know a motive and I had to know a killer, and in a cockeyed way I now knew both. The motive was whatever my mystery man wanted me to hand over to him. The killer was my mystery man. All I had to do was fill in the blanks.

What the hell was the stuff? Something worth money, but something you needed the right connections to handle properly. It could be dope or it could be spy secrets or it could be blackmail information or it could be. . . .

To hell with it. It could be anything.

There was no way to get a line on the package, no way to figure out why Sheila Kane had a hole in her head. There was no way to dope out the name and face that went with the raspy voice I'd talked to, no way to figure out how he'd connected me with Sheila. I might get something from Enright, but I wasn't seeing him until two-thirty and I had a few hours to kill. The only open avenue of approach was Sheila herself . . . what had Jack told me about her?

Damned little. She wasn't from New York, and if she knew a soul in town Jack didn't know about it. But she might have had something to do with the theater. Maybe.

And that much would fit in with the young-and-almost-innocent small-town girl on the loose in the big city. That type is drawn to the grease paint circuit like moths to a flame.

Not Broadway, not the way I saw it. Not the bright lights and the high-priced tickets. Sheila would have been more likely to have made her small inroads on the off-Broadway scene, where Equity minimum is a hot $45 a week and the ars comes gratis artist.

Which meant I should call Maddy Parson.

I had to look her number up in my notebook—it had been a long time. Then I picked up the damned phone again and dialed a Chelsea number. While the phone rang three times I thought about Madeleine Parson, a small and slender brunette with the kind of oval face and long neck that Modigliani would have loved to paint. Not a pretty girl by Hollywood's silly standards. A very beautiful one by mine.

An actress. An undiscovered thing who earned her forty-five bucks a week when she was lucky enough to catch a part and who prayed that whatever turkey she was in would run twenty weeks to put her in line for unemployment insurance when it finally gave up the ghost and folded. A girl who loved the theater with a capital T; a girl who waited for the one big break and who had fun while she waited. Not a Bohemian; not a fraud. An actress.

She answered midway through the fourth ring. Her hello was heartbreakingly hopeful.

"Relax," I told her. "Not an agent, not a producer, not a director. Just a dilettante."

27

"Ed! Ed London!" She sounded delighted. But that's the trouble with theater people. They're on stage twenty-four hours a day. It's hard to tell what's real.

"Are you working these days, Maddy?"

"Are you dreaming, Ed? I've had nibbles. Grinnell was going to cast me for the Agatha part in 'A Sound of Distant Drums' but the angel decided that oil stocks looked better than off-Broadway ventures. Then I ran second in the last three auditions. But they don't pay off for second place."

"Then you're free tonight?"

"As the air we breathe. Why?"

"I'd like to see you. I'll buy you a dinner and we'll talk far into the night. Sound good?"

"Sounds too good," she said. "So good there's a catch in it somewhere. Is this purely pleasure or is there some business on the agenda?"

I found myself smiling. "A little business, Maddy. We'll play questions and answers."

"I thought we would."

"No good?"

I could see her faking a pout into the telephone. "Well," she said, "I'd like to think you want to see me for my charm and beauty alone. But I don't really mind. I'll make you pay dearly for my company, sirrah. I'll force you to buy me a very expensive steak with at least two cocktails beforehand. To teach you a lesson."

"It's deductible. Seven o'clock all right?"

"I'll be too hungry by then. Make it six-thirty?"

We made it six-thirty. I told her I'd pick her up, then hung up and got out of the apartment. All that talk about steak had me hungry. I went down the block for a belated breakfast.

The air was warm outside and the waitress at the little restaurant was cheerful. I had shirred eggs and chicken livers with two cups of coffee. Real coffee, not instant. It was so good I almost forgot about the dead girl I'd dropped in Central Park and the raspy-voiced man who wanted to kill me.

Jack Enright's office was on Park Avenue at the corner of Eighty-eighth. A towering brick building. The liveried doorman opened my cab door, then hurried to yank open the building door for me. I walked straight to Jack's office on the first floor in the rear. I knew the way.

The receptionist looked as though someone had starched her to match her bright white uniform. She smiled at me without showing a single tooth and asked me who I was. I told her.

She repeated my name twice to commit it to memory. Then she got up from a blonde free-form desk and vanished through a heavy windowless door. I stood by her desk and studied the glut of patients waiting for the doctor. A sallow little man squinted through bifocals at the 'New Yorker.' Appropriately, a pregnant young woman had her nose buried in 'Parent's Magazine.' Four or five others sat around in the overstuffed chairs and stared at each other and at me. Their stares were pure envy when the woman in white came back and announced that the great man would see me.

I went through the door she pointed at, walked down a little hallway to Jack's private office. He was sitting behind a massive leather-topped wooden desk. Bookshelves which held medical texts and a smattering of classics lined the walls. There was a set of Trollope bound in morocco and a good Dickens in buckram.

A chair waited for me at the side of the desk. A pony of brandy was on the desk-top in front of the chair.

He said: "Courvoisier. Is it all right?"

It was more than all right. I took a sip and felt the taste buds on my tongue enjoying themselves.

"Well?"

I set down the glass and shrugged. "You're pretty well out of it," I said. "For the time being they've got nothing to tie you in."

"Thank God."

"But not completely out of it. As long as the killer's free, there's a chance that you'll get dragged into the picture. The police won't let go of it for awhile. The papers are playing with it. I saw a copy of the *Post* on the

29

way over. The early edition. A sex angle, a pretty girl, a shooting-and-dumping. It makes nice copy."

He nodded. "And you're going to look for the murderer?"

"I have to." I started to tell him I'd spoken to the killer, then changed my mind. "I came here to ask you some questions, Jack. I need a lot of answers."

"What do you want to know?"

"Everything you know. Everything, whether it seems important to you or not. People she knew, places she went to, anything she ever mentioned or did that'll give me a place to start digging. Whatever it is, I want to know about it."

I fished a pipe out of one pocket and a tobacco pouch from another. While I filled and lit the pipe he sat at his desk and thought. He ran the fingers of one hand through his dark hair. He drummed the leather desk-top with the fingers of the other hand. I shook out my match and dropped it into a heavy brass ashtray. He looked down at the match, then back at me.

"There's not a hell of a lot to tell, Ed. I've been trying to figure out how I could have been so damned close to a girl and know so little about her. She was from some little town in the sticks. Pennsylvania, I think. Maybe Ohio. I don't remember. She never mentioned her parents. If she had any brothers or sisters I never heard about them."

"Anything about the town?"

"Not a thing. That's how it went, Ed . . . when she was with me she was a girl without a past. She acted as if . . . as if she hadn't existed until we met."

I looked at him. "Isn't that a little romantic?"

"You know what I mean. She never mentioned anything that happened before we started our . . . affair. Here's an example—she came to me thinking she was pregnant. But she never mentioned any other man, or that there had been other men. Sometimes I felt I was only seeing a small part of her."

"The part she wanted you to see?"

"Maybe. She was like an iceberg. I saw the part above the water line."

30

I drew on the pipe, sipped more of the cognac. "Then let's forget her past," I said. "She's what you said. A girl without a past."

"And without a future. Ed—"

He was loosening up. "Steady," I said. "Let's take it from another angle. She must have had some friends in town, a guy or a girl she saw when you weren't around. And she couldn't have spent twenty-four hours a day in the apartment."

"You're probably right, but—"

"You mentioned something about show business. Was she looking for a part in a play? Hungry for bright lights?"

"I don't think so." He paused. "It was just an impression I got, Ed. Something in the way she talked and acted. Nothing concrete, nothing you could put your finger on. Just a vague notion, that's all."

"Then she didn't talk about it?"

"Not directly."

I was getting tired of it. "Damn it, what in hell did you talk about? You didn't discuss past or present or future. You didn't talk about her friends or her family or anything at all. Did you spend every damn minute in the hay?"

His mouth fell open and his face turned redder than blood. He looked as though he'd been kicked in the stomach.

"I'm sorry," I said honestly. "It came out wrong."

He nodded very slowly. "We talked," he said. "We talked about art and literature and the state of the universe. We had deep philosophical discussions that would have fit in perfectly in a Village coffee house. I could tell you a lot about her, Ed. She's an interesting person. Was an interesting person. It's hard to keep the tenses straight, hard to remember that she's dead."

He got up and came out from behind the desk. He started walking around the office, clenching and unclenching his fingers, pacing like a lion in a tiny cage. I didn't say anything.

"She preferred Brahms to Wagner and Mozart to Haydn. She didn't like stereo because you have to sit in

31

one spot to listen to it and she likes—liked—to move around. She wasn't religious exactly but she believed in God. A vague God who created the universe and then let it run by itself. She preferred long novels to short ones because once she got interested in a set of characters she wanted to spend some time with them."

He put out one cigarette and lit another. "She liked the color red," he went on. "One time I bought her a loud red-plaid bathrobe and she loved to lounge around the apartment in it. She liked good food—she was a hopeless cook but she liked to fool around in the kitchen. One night she broiled steaks for the two of us and we opened a bottle of '57 Beaujolais and ate by candlelight. I can tell you a million things like that, Ed. Nothing about her past, nothing about what she did or who she did it with. But I could fill volumes with the sort of person she was."

There was nothing to say because he couldn't have heard me. He was wrapped up in memories of a girl he would never see again, a girl he had loved. I wondered how he could be the kind of person he was, able to turn emotions on and off so easily. From Devoted Husband to Ardent Lover in nothing flat, and back again. He said he loved Kaye and I believed him. And I believed he loved Sheila.

"Let's try another angle," I suggested. "I know you don't want to hash over it. But let's go back to the apartment. Yesterday, when you found the body."

"She was dead." His voice was empty. "That's all . . . she was dead."

"I mean—"

A long sigh. "I know what you mean. Hell, what's the point? You saw everything I saw. You were there, weren't you? What more is there to say?"

"We saw it through different eyes. You may have caught something that I missed."

"I don't think so. I didn't see much of anything, Ed. Just her, dead. Everything was a mess and she was in the middle of it. I looked at the apartment and wondered what cyclone had hit it. I looked at her and I felt sick. I ran like a bat out of hell and went straight to you and . . . what's the matter?"

"The apartment," I snapped at him. "You said it was messy."

He looked at me strangely. "Sure," he said. "Hell, you saw it. Chairs knocked over, papers all over the floor—either she put up a fight or the bastard who killed her turned the place upside-down. You must have . . . what's wrong? Why are you staring like that?"

FOUR

I TOLD him why I was staring at him. I told him just how the apartment had looked, just how neat it had been. I watched him while I talked. His eyes were open wide and his mouth was open wider. My description of neatness was as jarring to him as his talk of disorder was to me.

"God," he said finally. "Then you didn't strip her."

I just looked at him.

"In the papers," he said. "I read that she was . . . half-naked when they found her. I thought you stripped her to keep them from identifying her from her clothes."

"I didn't have to. She wasn't wearing any."

He shook his head. "She was fully dressed when I found her, Ed. A sweater and a skirt, I think. I don't remember too well, my mind was swimming all over the place. But I would have remembered if she had been naked, wouldn't I?"

"It's a hard sight to forget."

"That's what I mean. When I read the paper . . . but I couldn't believe you stripped her, not really. I didn't think you would do something like that. It's sort of sacrilegious, taking the clothes from a dead body." He paused for breath. "Then I thought some sex fiend found her in the park before the police got there. Or that the papers were trying to make livelier copy out of it. Hell, I wasn't sure what to think. But if she was nude when you found her——"

I finished the sentence for him. "Then somebody got there after you left and before I arrived. That's what happened. Some clown cleaned her apartment from floor

34

to ceiling, took off her clothes and sneaked off into the night."

"But why?"

I couldn't answer that one.

"It's senseless," he exploded. "Nothing makes any sense. Killing Sheila didn't make any sense and neither does any of the rest of it. It's crazy."

He looked ready to blow up. I said: "Physician, heal thyself," and pointed to the bottle of Courvoisier. He poured us each a shot of brandy and we drank it.

I got out of there as fast as I could, but first I made him give me the only picture he had of the dead girl. I wanted to show it to Maddy. I put it in my wallet, said something cheerful to him, and left him to his patients.

The sallow little man peered myopically at me over his 'New Yorker,' the expectant mother put her magazine on her ample belly, and all of them looked happy as hell to see me. I said good-bye to the starched receptionist and walked out of the building.

The sun was shining and the air was clear and clean enough to breathe. I filled my lungs and headed for home. It was walking weather and I was glad—I was sick of sitting around waiting for things to happen. The walk gave me something to do, anyway. I winked at pretty girls and one or two of them even smiled back.

I didn't notice anybody following me. But that may have been because I didn't look.

Maybe I should have.

I didn't hear the bullet until it passed me.

I was in my building, on the way up the stairs. When I was a few steps from the landing there was a loud noise behind me. I was already falling on my face when the bullet buried itself in the wall. Plaster flew at my face.

Instinct said: Stay still, don't move. Instinct gave bad advice. Whoever he was, he was behind me and he was shooting at me and I made a hell of a good target.

But instinct's got a compelling voice. By the time I managed to spin around—it's tricky when you're on your

35

hands and knees on a staircase—he was gone. A door closed behind him and I looked at nothing.

"Mr. London?"

I looked up. Mrs. Glendower was leaning a gray head over the railing. Her expression was mildly puzzled.

"That wasn't a gunshot, was it? Or didn't you hear the noise?"

I got straightened out on my feet and tried to look sheepish. "Just a truck backfiring," I told her.

"It frightened me, Mr. London."

I managed to grin. "You're not the only one, Mrs. Glendower. It startled me so badly I nearly fell over. I've been nervous lately."

That was the perfect explanation as far as Mrs. Glendower was concerned. She smiled vaguely and pleasantly. Then she went away.

I went into my apartment and had a shot of cognac, then I went back into the hallway and looked at the hole in the wall. When I sighted from the bullet hole to the doorway I knew the gunman hadn't been trying to kill me at all. The bullet was way out of line. He must have missed me by five feet.

He could have been a lousy shot. But he didn't even make a second try—just one shot and away he went.

So it was a warning. A little message from the guy on the phone, the one with the raspy voice.

Fine.

I found a can of spackling paste in a drawer and patched up the hole in the wall, giving the bullet a permanent home. I let the paste dry, which didn't take long, and dabbed a little paint over it. It wasn't a perfect match but I didn't figure everybody in the world was going to come staring at my wall.

Then I went back inside and sat down.

It was an algebraic equation with too many unknowns. X was the killer, the voice on the phone. He shot the girl, searched the apartment and ran. Then Jack came in, looked around and ran. Then somebody else came, rearranged things, stripped the girl and ran. Then I came, carted off the body—and now everything was happening.

36

It didn't add up. And, like an algebraic equation, it wouldn't add up. Not until I knew all the unknowns.

In the meantime I had nothing to do, no place to go. There was a bullet in the wall outside my door and it wasn't worth the trouble to dig it out. What the hell was it going to prove? It might be a .32 or .38 slug. So what? I couldn't find out anything one way or the other, not that way.

So to hell with it.

I took a book from the bookcase and sat down with it. I read three pages, looked up suddenly and realized I didn't remember a word that I'd read. I put the book back on the shelf and poured more cognac. Nothing was working out.

And I was tied in deep. Jack was clear—I'd seen to that, rushing around like a goddam hero. But I was hanging by my thumbs. The bastard who shot a hole in Sheila knew who I was and where I lived and I didn't know a thing about him. And he had some damn fool idea that I had a package that he wanted. I was supposed to sell it to him.

There was only one catch. I didn't have it. I didn't even know what the hell it was.

Which complicated things. Jack was free and clear—he could go back to his wife, back to my sister. He could pretend that everything was all right with the world.

I couldn't.

I put music on the hi-fi and tried to listen to it. I hauled out my wallet and found the picture of Sheila Kane that Jack had given me. It was just a snapshot, probably taken with a box camera. The background—trees and open space—was out of focus. But the background wasn't important when you saw the girl.

Her long blonde hair was caught up in a pony tail. Her head was thrown back, her eyes bright. She was laughing. She wore a bulky turtle-neck sweater and a loose plaid skirt and she looked like the queen of the homecoming game.

I studied the picture and remembered everything Jack Enright had told me about her. I tried to imagine the kind of girl she must have been, tried to mesh that image with the image I got from the photograph. I came up with a person.

Poor Sheila, I kept thinking. Poor, poor Sheila.

"Poor Ed."

I looked across the table at Maddy Parson's pretty face. She was grinning at me over the brim of her second Daiquiri. Her eyes were sparkling. The two drinks had her high as a Chinese kite.

"Poor Ed," she said again. "You didn't know you'd get stuck for a dinner like this one. This is going to run you twenty dollars before we get out of here."

"It's worth it."

"I hope so," she said. "I hope you have some darn good questions to ask."

"I hope you know the answers."

We were at McGraw's on Forty-fifth near Third. There are girls who prefer the haute cuisine of French cookery; there are girls who will go anyplace to eat as long as it's fashionable; there are girls who like to sample out-of-the-way restaurants where not even the waiter can understand the menu. And there are still other girls—a few of them, anyhow—who like lean red meat and plenty of it with a big baked potato on the side. Maddy Parson belonged in the last group and that explains our presence at McGraw's.

McGraw's is a steakhouse. Which is a little like saying that the Grand Canyon is a hole in the ground. It's true enough but it doesn't tell the whole story. McGraw's is an institution.

The front window facing out on Forty-fifth Street opens on a cold room where hunks of steak hang and ripen. In the dining room the decor is unobtrusive nineteenth-century American male—heavy oak panelling, a thick wine-red carpet, massive leather chairs. They don't have a menu. All you do is tell your white-haired waiter how you want your sirloin and what you're drinking with it. If you don't order your meat rare he looks unhappy. We didn't disappoint the old gentleman.

"It's been a long time," Madeleine Parson was saying. "Almost too long. I don't know where to start talking."

38

"Start with yourself."

She rolled her eyes. "An actor's lot is not a happy one. Nor is an actress'. I almost took a job, Ed. Can you imagine that? Not even a semi-theatrical job that lets you kid yourself along. All the girls do that. They sell tickets in a box office or follow a producer around and sharpen his pencils for him and think they're learning the business from the ground up. But I almost took a job selling hats. Can you imagine that? I thought to myself how easy it would be, just sell hats and earn a steady $72.50 a week before taxes and move up gradually, maybe be a buyer in time, and—"

She saw the expression on my face. Her eyes danced and she laughed. "Then my agent called me and told me Schwerner was auditioning for 'Love Among The Falling Stars' and I stuffed my mental hats into a mental hatbox and went away singing. I didn't get the part. I read miserably and it wasn't right for me to begin with. But I forgot all about selling hats."

"You'll get your break, Maddy."

"Of course I will. And I'll need it, Ed. I came to New York ready to take Broadway by storm. I was the best damn actress in the country and it was only a question of time before the rest of the world figured it out for themselves. And I was lousy, Ed. I'm not too good even now. Hayes and Cornell have nothing to worry about."

Her eyes were challenging. "And suppose I don't get that damn break, Ed? Then what do I do? Sell hats?"

I shook my head. "Meet some lucky guy and marry him. Live in a house and make babies. It's better than selling hats."

"Uh-huh." A smile that was not altogether happy spread slowly over her face. "It's funny, Ed. I had an offer not long ago."

"That's not funny. You should get lots of offers."

"This one was different. He wasn't a jerk or a square or a Philistine. He was a hell of a nice guy. Thirty-six years old, associate editor at a properly respectable publishing house, with a yen to buy one of those wonderful stone houses in Bucks County and fill it with children. He was a good talker and a good listener and good in

39

bed. God, I'm talking like a successful actress, telling one man what another one's like in bed. I hate me when I talk like that. But you know what I'm driving at, Ed. He was nice. I think you would have liked him—I know I did, and he wanted me to marry him."

"But you didn't."

"Nope."

"How come?"

She closed her eyes. "I thought about being married," she said softly. "And I thought about waking up every single morning with somebody else in bed with me. And I thought maybe one day I'd want to take a trip somewhere, or maybe I'd get sick of the house and want to live someplace else, or I'd meet some guy and get an itch to go out with him and find out what he was like. And I thought that I'd have to pass up all these things, and how it would be, being tied to one man and one home and one way of life that you live with until you die. So much freedom out the window, so much responsibility around your neck like the albatross in that poem everybody had to read in the tenth grade. And I thought, God, you'd have to love somebody a hell of a lot to put up with such a load of crap. And I just didn't love him that much. I loved him, but not enough."

I didn't say anything. The oval face was a mask now. The eyes were opaque. A good actress can conceal emotions, just as she can portray them.

"So here I am," she said. "Free and white and twenty-seven. That's not so young any more, Ed. Pretty soon some other nice guy'll ask me to follow him to the nearest altar and I won't love him enough either and it won't be so important any more and I'll say yes. I'm a tragic figure, Ed. Too old to play games and too young to admit it. It's a hell of a thing." She looked over her shoulder and smiled. "Here come the steaks," she said. "Now we can stop talking."

The steaks came and we stopped talking. Conversation is the wrong accompaniment to a meal at McGraw's. The meat has to be approached quietly, reverently. Talk comes later. We attacked the steaks like tigers. They were black with charcoal on the outside and raw in the middle and nothing ever tasted better.

Afterward she had Drambuie and I had cognac. I leaned forward to light her cigarette, then put the match to my pipe. I watched her draw the smoke deep into her lungs and let it escape slowly between slightly parted lips. She used very little lipstick. Her shade was a very dark red.

"What time is it, Ed?"

"A few minutes past nine."

"God! That late?"

"I didn't pick you up until quarter of seven. It took us another fifteen minutes to get out of your apartment. We had to wait for a table. Two drinks before dinner, a leisurely meal——"

"The time flew." She sighed. "Well, I suppose it's time for the business side of things. You have questions to ask me, sir. Want to ask them here or go elsewhere?"

"Elsewhere sounds good," I said. "Where do you want to go?"

"Obviously a very exclusive and most expensive cafe in the east Fifties, of course. That's what I should suggest. But I'm going to be a considerate young lady and a forward wench at the same time. Let's go back to my apartment."

"Fine."

"After all," she said, "you've been there before."

She lived in a third-floor loft on West Twenty-fourth just east of Eighth. Her building had been condemned years ago and it wasn't legal to live there, but Maddy and the landlord had taken care of all that. According to the lease, she used the loft to give acting lessons and didn't live there at all. The landlord paid the trustworthy firemen so much a month and everybody was happy. Maddy would go on living there until the building came down around her little ears.

A rusty machine shop took up the ground floor of the old brick building. An ancient palmist and crystal-gazer named Madame Sindra held court on the second floor. We climbed to the third floor on an unlit and shaky wooden staircase. I stood by while Maddy unlocked the door.

The apartment inside looked as though it belonged in a different building in a different part of town. The living room was huge, with a false fireplace along one wall and a massive studio couch on the other. All the furniture was expensive-looking, but Maddy had picked it up, a little at a time, at the University Place auction houses and she made a few dollars go a long way. There were a few bookcases, all of them crammed with paperbacks and covered with Moselle bottles topped with candle-drippings.

Now she waved small hands at everything. "Be it ever so affected, there's no place like home. Sit down, Ed. Relax. I don't have a thing to drink, but relax anyway."

I sat down on the couch. She kicked off her shoes and curled up next to me with her legs tucked neatly under her pretty little behind. "Now," she said. "Fire away, Mr. London, sir. Be a devastatingly direct detective and detect like mad. I'll oblige with all my heart."

I took Sheila's picture from my wallet. I looked at it and she peered over my shoulder.

"Who's she?"

"Her name's Sheila Kane. Does it ring a bell?"

"I don't think so. Should it?"

"Just a hunch," I said. "Somebody thought she might be a show biz nut one way or another."

"An actress?"

"Maybe. Or some outsider in the theatrical in-group. Or the guy who told me this has rocks in his head, which isn't impossible. I had an idea you might have run into her somewhere."

"The name doesn't sound familiar," She tossed her head. "But then one meets so many exciting people in this mad and wonderful life——"

I laughed. "Give it a good look," I suggested. "You might have met her without an introduction. Make sure."

She craned her neck to look more closely over my shoulder and her soft black hair brushed my face. I could smell the sweetness of her. She wore no perfume, only the healthy vibrance of a well-scrubbed young woman. Which was enough.

"No pony tail," she said suddenly. "Her hair loose and flowing. And this must have been taken awhile ago, if it's the same gal. She didn't look so damned Betty Co-ed when I saw her. And her name wasn't Sheila Kane."

"Are you sure?"

"Almost. Gosh, you're excited, aren't you? It's nice to see a real detective in action."

I growled at her. "Talk."

"Not much to talk about." She shrugged her pretty shoulders. "I don't know much. I met her only once and that was about . . . oh, say six or seven weeks ago. I could find out the exact date easily enough. It was the night 'Hungry Wedding' opened. Did you see it?"

I hadn't.

"You didn't have much chance. It closed after five performances, to the surprise of practically no one and to the delight of many. It was a gold-plated turkey."

"You weren't in it, were you?"

"No such luck. That's usually the kind of show I wind up in, the type that fights to last a week. But I missed this one. Anyway, I was tight with a few kids in the cast and I got an invite to the cast party. It was sort of a wake. Everybody in the show knew they were going to get a roasting. But no actor passes up a party with free drinks. We all got quietly loaded."

"And Sheila Kane was there?"

"With one of the angels," she said. "She wasn't an actress. She waltzed in on the arm of a very grim-looking man with a cigar in his mouth. His name was Clay and her name was Alicia and that's all I found out about either of them. I didn't particularly want to know more, to tell you the truth. He looked like a Hollywood heavy and she looked like Whore Row Goes To College and I just wasn't interested."

"Clay——"

"Clay and Alicia, and don't ask me her last name or his first name. I don't know how much money he wasted on the show but he didn't seem to give a damn. He smoked his cigars and nursed one glass of sour red wine and ignored everybody. She spent her time watching everybody very carefully. Like a rich tourist taking a walk on the Bowery, curious about everything but careful not to get her precious hands dirty. I took an instant dislike to her. I suppose it was bitchy of me but that's the way I am. I make quick judgments. I didn't like her at all."

"Anyone else with either of them?"

"Not that I noticed. And no, I don't remember who the other backers were. Lee Brougham produced the play—he could tell you who put up the money, I suppose. Unless he thought you were trying to steal his angels for a dog of your own. But he'll be tough to find. I heard he went to the coast. You can't blame him after 'Hungry Wedding.' A genuinely terrible play. An abortion."

She didn't have anything more to tell me. She hadn't seen the girl again, never heard anything more about her. I tried to fit the new picture with what I knew about Sheila Kane. Now her name was Alicia, and she sounded a little less like Jack Enright's mistress, a little less like the girl in the snapshot.

And I had another name now. Mr. Clay. Joe Clay? Sam Clay? Tom, Dick or Harry Clay?

To hell with it. It was another scrap and it would fit into place eventually. In the meantime we could switch to another topic of conversation.

But I forgot I was talking to Maddy Parson.

"Now," she said dramatically, "give."

I tried to look blank.

"It is now my turn to play detective, Mr. London, sir. If you think you can pump me blind without telling me a damn thing——"

"Pump you dry, you mean."

"That sounds dirty, sort of. And don't change the subject. You are now going to tell me all about Sheila or Alicia or whoever the hell she is. Come clean, Mr. London, sir."

"Maddy——"

"About the girl," she said heavily. "Talk."

I said: "She's dead, Maddy."

"Oh. I sort of thought so. Now I'm sorry I didn't like her. I mean——"

44

"I know."

"Tell me the whole thing, Ed. I'll be very quiet and I won't repeat a thing to a soul. I'll be good. But tell me."

I told her. There was no reason to keep secrets from her. She wasn't involved, didn't know any of the people involved, and made a good sounding board for the ideas that were rattling around in my head. I gave her the full summary, from the minute Jack Enright walked through my door to the moment I picked her up for dinner. I didn't leave anything out.

She shivered properly when I told her how I got shot at. She made a face when I described the scene in the blonde girl's apartment. And she listened intently all the way through.

"So here you are," she said finally. "Hunting a killer and dodging him at the same time. You think Clay's the killer?"

I shrugged. "He looks as good as anybody else, but I don't know who he is."

"He looked capable of murder. Be careful, Ed."

"I'm always careful. I'm a coward."

She grinned at me. I grinned back, and we stood up together, both grinning foolishly. Somewhere along the way the grins gave way to deep long looks. Her eyes were not opaque at all now. I stared into them.

Then all at once she was in my arms and I was stroking silky hair. Her face buried itself against my chest and my arms were filled with the softness of her.

She pulled away from me. Her voice was very small. "I'm going to be forward again," she said. "Very forward. You're not going home now, Ed. I don't want you to go."

"I don't want to go."

"I'm glad," she said, taking my hand. "I'm very glad, Ed. And I don't think we should stay in here. I think we should go to the bedroom."

We started for the bedroom.

"It's right through that door," she said, pointing. "But you know that. After all, you've been there before."

45

FIVE

SHE was soft and warm and sweet. She moved beside me and her lips nuzzled my ear. "Don't go," she whispered. "Stay all night. I'll make breakfast in the morning. I make good coffee, Ed."

I drew her close and buried my face in the fragrance of her hair. Her body pressed against mine. Sleep was drowning me, dragging me under. The bed was warm, too warm to get out of. Sheila Kane and Jack Enright and a man called Clay were dull and trivial, a batch of mute ciphers swimming in charcoal gray water. I wanted to let them drown, to wink the world away with Maddy's fine female body beside me.

Something stopped me. "I've got to go," I said.

"Don't, Ed. See how shameless I am? Every sentence ends with a proposition. But stay here. It gets so lonely in this bed. It's a big bed. I rattle around in it all by myself. Don't go."

She didn't say anything while I slipped out of bed and fumbled around for my clothes. I leaned over to kiss her cheek and she didn't move a muscle or speak a word. Then, while I was tying my shoelaces, she sat upright in the bed and talked to me. A half-light from the living room bathed her in yellow warmth. The sheet had fallen away from her small breasts and she looked like a primitive goddess with wild hair and sleepy eyes.

"Be careful, Ed. I'm not kidding; I like you; I like having you around, be careful, please. I don't like the way everything sounds. These people are dangerous. My God, one of them tried to kill you——"

"It was just a warning."

"He shot at you. He could have killed you."

46

"Please don't worry."

"Of course I'll worry. It's a woman's prerogative to worry—you ought to know that. Worrying makes me feel all female and motherly and everything. If I only knew how to knit I'd make you a nice warm sweater. A warm wool sweater with a bullet-proof lining. Would you like that?"

I grinned. "Sounds good."

Her tone turned serious. "You better call me tomorrow, you bastard. Otherwise I'll get mad. When I get mad I'm hell on wheels, Ed. There's no telling what I might do. I could sic the Mafia on you or something." She frowned. "So call me."

"I will."

"But not before noon." A low sigh. "I like to sleep late. I wish you could stay with me, Ed. We'd both sleep late and then I'd cook breakfast and feel as domestic as a pair of bedroom slippers. Maybe I'll knit you a pair of bedroom slippers."

I laughed.

"Now kiss me good-bye. That's right. Now get the hell out of here before I start bawling, because this whole scene is so touching I can't take it. Did you know I can cry on cue? It's a valuable talent. Good-bye, Ed. And be careful. And call me. And . . ."

I kissed her again. Her lips were very soft, and when I kissed her she closed her eyes. Then I left her there and went out into the night.

On the way home the streets were almost empty. I took Eighth Avenue uptown to Columbus Circle where it turned into Central Park West, then angled the Chevy through the park and came out at Fifth and 67th. The ride through the park got to me—I remembered another trip the night before when I had a passenger in the car. A dead one.

I drove straight to the garage and got set for a session of playing straight man to the kid with the acne. It turned out to be his night off, which was wonderful. The guy taking over for him was a nautical type with a lantern jaw and tattooed forearms. One of the tattoos was a naked girl with impossible breasts; another I noticed was an anchor with 'Mother' etched across it. He was long and stringy and short of speech and I couldn't have been happier. I gave him the Chevy and walked home.

It was maybe two-thirty. The air was clear and it had a chill to it. My footsteps were hollow against the backdrop of a silent night. A taxi took a corner and its tires squealed. I looked around and made sure nobody was following me. It was a good thing. My building was solidly built, but too many holes in the wall could weaken it.

The brownstone waited for me. I unlocked the outer door and took the stairs two at a time. I stopped in front of my door, stuffed tobacco into a pipe and lit it. Then I stuck my key in the lock and opened the door.

I flicked on the light and saw him. He was sitting in my chair smoking a cigarette. He was neither smiling nor frowning. He looked nervous.

"Please close the door," he said. "And please sit down, Mr. London. I have to talk with you."

He was holding a small pistol in his left hand. It was not aimed at me. He held it almost apologetically, as if to say that he was sorry he had to hold a gun on me and he'd at least be enough of a gentleman to point it somewhere else.

I closed the door and moved into the center of the living room. He gestured with the gun, indicating a chair, and I sat in it.

"I'm very sorry about this," he said. "I really wanted to find the briefcase in your apartment and be gone before you returned. Wishful thinking, I fear. A very thorough search revealed only that your taste in music and in literature is not coincident with mine. You prefer chamber music while I tend to favor crashing orchestral pieces. But the furnishings here are marvellous, simply marvellous. This rug is a Bokhara, isn't it?"

I nodded at him. He was a very small and very neat man. He wore black Italian loafers of pebble-grain leather with pointed toes. His suit was lamp-black, continental cut. His tie was a very proper foulard and his shirt was crisply white. There was something indefinably foreign

48

about him. His eyes had a vaguely oriental cast and his complexion was dark, close to olive. I couldn't pin down his accent but he had one. His head and face were round, his hair jet black and he was going bald in front. This made his face even rounder.

"We're both reasonable men," he said. "Rational individuals. I'm sure you realize I wouldn't have broken in if I could have avoided it. I did use a device which opened your lock without damaging it."

"Thanks."

He almost smiled. "You resent me, don't you? It's easy to understand. But I hope to conquer your resentment. Since we'll be doing business together, Mr. London . . ."

He let the sentence trail off. "You're way ahead of me," I said. "You know my name."

"You may call me Peter Armin. It will be meaingless to you, but it's as good a name as any."

I didn't say anything.

"To return to the subject," he said. "The briefcase. It's really no good to you and I'm prepared to pay very well for it. A simple business transaction. I have a use for it and you do not. That's a natural foundation for economic cooperation, don't you think?"

Then the missing item was a briefcase. I wondered what was in it.

I said: "You're not the only one who wants it."

"Of course not. If I were, you'd sell it to me for next to nothing. But I'll pay handsomely for it. Five thousand dollars."

"No sale."

He shrugged. I caught a whiff of his cigarette. It smelled like Turkish or Egyptian tobacco. "I don't blame you," he said. "I was being cheap and that's indecent. The briefcase is worth ten thousand dollars to me. I cannot afford to pay more and wouldn't if I could. That's my offer. Is it a good one?"

"Probably. What if I say I don't have the briefcase?"

"I don't think I would believe you."

"Why not?"

His smile spread. "It's hardly logical. After all, Mr.

Bannister doesn't have the briefcase. I'm certain of that. And I'm very glad of it as well. He's an unpleasant man, Mr. Bannister is. Uncouth and uncultured. Boorish. You wouldn't like him at all, Mr. London. You may dislike me, but you'd detest Mr. Bannister."

I looked at the gun in his left hand. It was a Beretta. A .22-calibre gun. I wondered if he killed Sheila with it.

"Bannister doesn't have it," Armin went on. "He wants it but he doesn't have it. And I doubt that he'd be willing to pay as much for it as I am. He'd probably try to take it away from you by force. A crude man. So you should sell it to me, you see."

"Suppose I don't have it?"

"But you must. You were at the girl's apartment. So was the briefcase. It's not there now because you have it. It follows."

"Like night follows day. Suppose someone else was at her place?"

He shrugged again. His face was very sad now. "I was there," he said. "Really, I'm in a position to know that I don't have the thing. If I had it I wouldn't be here, much as I enjoy your company. And Mr. Bannister was at the girl's apartment. But he doesn't have it either. That leaves you."

"Eeny meeny miny moe?"

"More or less. Really, there's no reason for you to deny that you have the case. It's no use whatsoever to you, whereas no man lives who can't find a use for ten thousand dollars. And I need the case very badly. Desperately, you might say. Can't we do business?"

I relit my pipe and looked at Armin. I wondered who and what the hell he was. French or Greek or Italian or Spanish or Cuban. I couldn't place the accent.

"Fine," I said. "I've got the briefcase. So what's in it?"

He stroked his chin. "If you have the case and know what's inside," he said, "it would be a waste of time to tell you. If you have the case and do not understand the significance of the contents, it would be foolish to tell you. And there must be a chance in a thousand that you are telling the truth, that you do not have the case. Why in the world should I tell you?"

"Who's Bannister? Who are you?"

He smiled.

"Who killed the girl? Why was she killed?"

He didn't answer.

"Who shot at me?"

He shrugged.

I let out a sigh. "You're wasting your time," I told him. "And mine. I don't have the case."

"Then it's not for sale?"

"Take it any way you want it. I don't have the briefcase and it's not for sale."

His sigh was very unhappy. He got to his feet, still holding the gun loosely in his hand. "If you want more money, I really can't help you. Ten thousand is my top price. I erred in offering five thousand first. I'm not generally that type of businessman. I quote one price and it is a firm price." He managed a shrug. "Perhaps you'll reconsider while there's still time. You may call me any hour, day or night. Let me give you my card."

His right hand dipped into his inside jacket-pocket. We were both on our feet and the gun was pointed at the floor.

I picked that moment to hit him.

My right hand sank into his gut and my left hand closed around the gun. I hit him hard, harder than I planned, and he collapsed like a blown-out tire and folded up into the chair. The gun stayed in my hand, a light and cool piece of metal. I switched it to my right hand and pointed it at him.

His shoulders sagged and his eyes were pools of misery. He was massaging himself where I hit him. His face was a mask of infinite disappointment.

"You hit me," he said thoughtfully. "Now why did you do that?"

I didn't have an answer handy. "The briefcase," I snapped. "Tell me about it. Tell me about yourself and about Bannister. Tell me who killed the girl."

He sighed again. "You don't seem to understand," he said sadly. "We're at a stalemate. We should be co-operating and we're at odds. I didn't threaten you with the gun, Mr. London, for the simple reason that it would

51

have accomplished nothing. Now you have the gun and you can't do a thing with it. Ask me all the questions you wish. I won't answer them. What can you do? Shoot me? Beat me? Call the police? You won't do any of those things. It's a stalemate, Mr. London."

The annoying thing was that he as right all the way. I stood there with the gun in my hand and felt like a clown. I was sorry I hit him. It was a waste of time, for one thing. For another, I was beginning to like the little weasel. I tried to picture myself beating him up or shooting him or calling the cops. The picture didn't look too sensible.

"You see what I mean, Mr. London. We're similar men, you and I. Neither of us is unnecessarily violent. In that respect Mr. Bannister has the advantage on us. He would beat us or have us beaten purely as a matter of course if we stood in his way. That's why you and I should be allies. But perhaps you'll come to your senses."

He stood up stiffly, still holding himself where I slugged him. Once again his right hand dipped into his pocket. This time he came up with a pigskin pocket secretary. He flipped it open and took out a card which he handed to me. I read: Peter Armin . . . Hotel Ruskin . . . Room 1104 . . . OXford 2-1560.

"The Ruskin," he said. "On West Forty-fourth Street. I'll be there for the next several days."

I put the card in my pocket. He stood still and I realized I was still pointing the gun at him. I lowered it.

"Mr. London," he said. He lowered his eyes. "May I have my gun back?"

"So you can shoot me with it?"

"Hardly. I just want my gun."

"You don't need it," I told him. "You're not a violent man."

"I might have to defend myself."

"You're not the only one. Somebody shot at me today."

"Mr. Bannister?"

"Maybe. I think I'll hold onto your gun. I might need it sooner or later." I shrugged. "I didn't invite you here, anyway."

His smile returned. "As you wish," he said. "I have another at the hotel."

"A thirty-two? The one you shot the girl with?"

He laughed now. "I didn't kill her," he said. "And if I had, I'd hardly hold onto the gun. No, the other is a Beretta, the mate to the one you're holding. Good night, Mr. London."

I didn't move. He turned his back on me and walked past me to the door. He left the apartment quickly and closed the door after himself. I listened to his footsteps on the stairway, heard the front door slam behind him. I walked to the window and watched him cross the street and get into a maroon Ford a year or two old. He drove away.

Something kept me at the window, waiting for him to circle the block and come back for me. This didn't happen. After ten minutes, with no sight of him or his car, I went to the door and slid the bolt into place. The lock itself wasn't doing me a hell of a lot of good lately.

I spilled cognac into a glass and drank it. I juggled names like Peter Armin and Bannister and Alicia and Sheila and Clay and I tried to fit them into the human equation along with S, Y and Z. Nothing added up, nothing took form.

At least I knew what we were looking for now. A briefcase—but it didn't do me a hell of a lot of good to know that. First I had to figure out what was in the case.

Which was a good question.

Anyway, it was a good thing I hadn't given in to temptation and spent the rest of the night with Maddy. I would have missed Armin's visit.

Or would I have? I couldn't help smiling. The funny little guy probably would have sat in the darkness all night long, waiting for me with the little toy gun in his hand.

I looked at the gun, smelled the barrel. It hadn't been fired recently. I stuck it in a drawer and went to bed.

SIX

I SAT in an overstuffed chair in the middle of a neat and spacious room. A healthy fire roared in the fireplace and animated figures of X, Y and Z danced in crackling flames. The man called Clay shuffled into the room with a girl on his arm. He wore a Broadway suit and a snap-brim hat. There was a cigar in the corner of his mouth and pale green smoke drifted from it to the ceiling. He did not have any eyes.

I looked from him to the girl. I saw she was a skeleton with long blonde hair. She wore only a pair of nylon stockings and a garter belt. She did a stripper's bump-and-grind, tossing loins of bone at me.

I turned and saw Bannister. He was built along the lines of an anthropoid ape. His arms were longer than his legs. He had a length of lead pipe in one hand and a baseball bat in the other. "The briefcase," he rasped. "The briefcase the briefcase the briefcase the briefcase."

I looked down. There was a briefcase on my lap. It smelled of good leather and death. I clutched it in both hands and hugged it to my chest.

When I looked up again Bannister had turned into Peter Armin. He was pointing a Beretta at the man called Clay, whose face had changed to Jack Enright's. "Help me, Ed," Jack was saying. And "Help me," choruse X, Y and Z. They were still dancing in the fireplace, skipping gaily in the flames.

Armin turned, pointed the Beretta at me. "I, Mr. London, am a reasonable man," he said. "And you, Mr. London, are a reasonable man. We are not men of violence."

Then he shot me.

54

I looked up at the skeleton. Her hair was black now and her face was Maddy Parson's face. She screamed a shrill, piercing scream. She stopped, then shrieked again.

● ● ●

The third scream wasn't a scream at all. It was the telephone ringing, ringing viciously, and it brought back reality in bits and pieces. I got oriented again—I was in bed, it was early morning, and the phone was going full blast. I picked up the receiver and growled at it.

"Ed? This is Jack, Ed."

I asked him what time it was. It was the first thing I thought of.

"Time? Eight or so, a few minutes after. Ed, I'm calling from a pay phone. Can we talk?"

"Yes," I said. "What's wrong?"

"They've identified her."

"They?"

"The police."

"They identified Sheila Kane?"

"That's right."

It didn't seem possible. I figured they might tag her eventually if they worked on it long enough, but it would be a few weeks, even with luck—not overnight.

"Do you have a newspaper handy, Ed?"

"I'll read it later," I told him. "Jack, you're in trouble. If they've got her labelled they'll have you in nothing flat. You better beat them to the punch. Get in touch with Homicide, tell them you're surrendering voluntarily, you didn't kill her, you're just guilty of withholding evidence. That way——"

"Ed."

I stopped.

"Ed, do you get the *Times*?"

"Sure, but——"

"It can explain better than I can. I'll hold the line. Get your newspaper and read the story. Check page 34— that's the second page of the second section. Go on— read it. Then you'll see what I mean."

I was too foggy to argue with him. I managed to get out

55

of bed, found a robe on a hook in the closet, slipped it on. I padded barefoot from the bedroom through the living room to the door, opened the door and picked up the paper. I carried it inside, shut the door and got rid of the first section on the way back to the phone. I ran my eyes over page 34 until I came to the right story. The headline said:

POLICE IDENTIFY CORPSE
FOUND IN CENTRAL PARK

The article ran seven paragraphs but the kicker was right there at the top in paragraph one. They had a make on the dead blonde, all right, but that was no reason for Jack to hand himself in at headquarters.

Not at all.

Because they had identified her as Alicia Arden, twenty-five, of 87 Bank Street in Greenwich Village. The identification was a pretty simple matter, too. Somebody sent her prints to the FBI's Washington office. Her prints were on file there—Alicia Arden had a record. She'd been arrested in Santa Monica four years back on a disorderly conduct charge, had drawn a suspended sentence and had vanished from the area—at least as far as the police records show.

The story ran downhill from there on to the finish. The possible identity of the killer was unknown. Clues were conspicuously absent. Miss Arden had no friends or relatives. Her Village apartment was one room plus a bath, and nobody in her building knew the first thing about her.

The police were pursuing all angles of the case thoroughly, according to the *Times* reporter. I read between the lines and saw that they were getting ready to write the murder off as unsolvable. A detective sergeant named Leon Taubler was quoted as saying that, although the girl hadn't been sexually molested, "It looks like a sex crime."

All the unsolved murders in Manhattan look like sex crimes. It helps the police and the tabloids at the same time. One hand washes the other.

I picked up the phone again. Jack's voice was hoarse. "You read the story? You see what I mean?"

I answered yes to both questions.

"I can't believe it," he said heavily. "They must have made a mistake."

"No mistake."

"But——"

"Fingerprints don't make mistakes," I said. "And even if they did, it's a little too much to expect both gals to be missing at the same time. There's no mistake, Jack."

"It doesn't seem possible."

"It does to me. Sheila—Alicia—was living two lives at once. I more or less figured that much last night. A girl I know recognized her picture, met her once at a party. She was using the Alicia name at the time. So the newspaper story wasn't as much of a shock to me as it was to you."

"Why would she give me a wrong name?"

"She went to you because she thought she was pregnant," I improvised. "She handed you a phony name automatically. Then she stayed with it. It was easier than admitting a lie."

There was a long pause. "What's disorderly conduct, Ed? What does it mean?"

"All things to all people. It's like vagrancy—a handy catch-all for the police. The New York cops use it for prostitutes. Easier to prove. God knows what it means in Santa Monica. Anything from keeping bad company to walking the streets in a tight skirt."

"You heard me talk about her. About the type of person she was. Did she sound like that newspaper story?"

"No."

"That just wasn't her, Ed. Maybe I didn't know who she was or where she came from, but I certainly knew the sort of girl she was. And, damn it, she wasn't a tramp!"

"Not when she was with you," I said.

"She was still the same person, wasn't she?"

"Not necessarily." I got a cigarette going and talked through a mouthful of smoke. "Look at it this way. She was living two lives. Part of the time she was Bank Street's

57

Alicia Arden and the rest of the time she was your girl Sheila. She probably had two personalities, one to go with each name. You must have represented a better way of life to her, Jack. You told me about the first time you took her to lunch, how she stood there like a kid with her nose against a candy-store window. It wasn't the luxury that excited her. It was the respectability."

"Is it so damned respectable to be a mistress?"

"It is if you used to be a prostitute."

"Ed——"

"Hang on a minute. You were a cushion, Jack. A security blanket. A nice decent guy with a nice clean safe apartment in the fabulous Fifties. She was a little girl up to her neck in trouble with a batch of very unpleasant people. Hell, she was in over her head—that's why she was killed. But when she was with you she could pin her hair up and relax. She could be calm and cool and cultured. She was in a very lovely dream world and life was good to her. Naturally she was a different person in that world. You made her that way."

"She seemed so honest, Ed."

"She was honest enough," I said. "She could have lied to you, could have invented a background for herself. Instead she left the past blank. That's honest, isn't it?"

"I suppose you're right. It's . . . hard to accept the whole mess, Ed. I still don't know what's happening. You know how I felt when I saw the story this morning? First I read the headline and thought the police would be breaking down my door any minute. Then I read the first paragraph and I thought: God, the girl was somebody else and Sheila is still alive. It took me a few minutes to come to my senses again."

I didn't say anything. Things were starting to take form in my mind and I wanted to get rid of Jack so that I could think straight. My human equation was setting itself up.

"You mentioned something about her being in over her head, Ed. Were you kidding?"

"No," I said.

"What's it all about?"

"I don't know. Did she ever mention anything to you about a briefcase?"

"A briefcase?"

"Yeah."

"No," he said. "Never."

"Ever see one around the apartment?"

"No. Why?"

"Just wondered," I said. "Look, you're free as green stamps now. If the police have her under one name they won't look for another. If they've nailed her to one address they won't worry about a missing girl on Fifty-first Street. You can stop worrying and start living. Like the books say."

For a moment or two he said nothing. Then: "I see. What do I do now?"

I frowned at the phone. "You pretend you're a family man," I said. "You take good care of your wife and your kids. You remove a lot of appendixes and split a lot of fees and have a ball."

"Ed——"

"Give my best to my sister," I told him. "So long."

I hung up on him before he could thank me or tell me anymore of his problems or do whatever he was going to do. He was out of it now and I was bored with him. He had his small fling, got into a mess, and I helped him get out of it smelling of roses—which was more than he deserved. And in return for that I was getting warned, shot at and generally annoyed.

I decided to send the bastard a bill.

I went down the street for breakfast because it was too damned early to try stomaching instant coffee. I read the rest of the Times with breakfast but couldn't keep my mind on what I was reading. I had the names of all the characters now and things were setting themselves up.

The human equation—X and Y and Z. X killed Sheila, Y cleaned up her apartment and Z had the briefcase.

And I had the names to fit the letters.

Peter Armin. I couldn't figure him for X, the killer. He just didn't fit there at all. And I knew that he didn't have the briefcase because he wouldn't go to such a hell of a lot of trouble to get it from me if he did. That put him in the Y position—the joker who straightened things up, stripped Sheila and otherwise tampered with the scenery. I couldn't figure out why—that would come later, with luck—but it was in character. He'd given my apartment a thorough search the night before without disturbing a thing. It stood to reason that he'd be equally considerate of Sheila's apartment.

That left X and Z. Now——

"Nice morning," the waitress said.

I looked up at her. "Is it? I hadn't noticed."

She started to laugh. I must have said something funny as hell because she was laughing hysterically. I tucked X and Z away for future reference, paid her, tipped her and went home.

I got there in time to answer the phone.

It was the man with the raspy voice again.

"You had time to think. Now you can go or get off the pot, London. How much?"

"How much for what?"

"The briefcase. Come on, quit stalling. What's the price?"

"I haven't got it," I said.

There was a pregnant pause. "That's your story? You haven't got it?"

"That's my story."

"One last chance," he said. His voice was supposed to sound coaxing. Try coaxing in a rasp. It doesn't come off. "One last chance, London. You're a smart boy. I play very rough. How much do you want for it?"

"Are you Bannister?"

"I'm Al Capone," he said. "What do you say, London?"

I said: "Go to hell, Al." And I hung up on him.

I made coffee, filled and lit a pipe, sat down to think. I was pretty sure it was Bannister on the phone. I was just as sure that Bannister was X—that he had killed Sheila-Alicia himself or had ordered the killing.

That left Z and it left Clay, so I put the two of them together. He was the one with the briefcase.

It played itself out that far and it hit a snag. I couldn't

carry it any further. It looked as though Sheila-Alicia had teamed up with Clay to pull something on Bannister. Or, as though, Sheila-Alicia had something Bannister wanted, and she gave it to Clay, and then Bannister killed her. But there wasn't much point in listing possibilities. First I needed more facts.

Like Bannister's name. Like Clay's name.

Like an idea of what was in the briefcase.

I gave up for the time being, picked up the phone again and gave Maddy a ring. It was too early to call her, too early for her to be properly awake. I could have been polite, waited a few hours to call her, but I didn't feel polite to begin with. Too many people had called me early in the morning for me to take anybody else's sleep into consideration.

Still, Maddy was special. And I felt guilty, expecting her to answer the phone with sleep coating her tongue and clogging her pores. She surprised me. Her hello was fresh and happy and very much awake.

"Sleep well?"

"It's Ed," she said gaily. "Hello, Ed. Yes, I slept well. Like a hibernating bear, sort of. Then I woke up and saw my shadow. Or is that with groundhogs? I guess it is. Anyway, I slept soundly and awoke bright-eyed and hungry. You missed a phenomenal breakfast, sir. Fresh orange juice and pancakes with real maple syrup and crisp bacon."

She said all this with one mouthful of air, then stopped and caught her breath. "And then it was all topped off with a phone call from you. How sweet! You're still alive!"

I laughed, picturing her in my mind. Her phone was by the side of her bed. She would be sitting on the edge of the bed with a cigarette in one hand and the phone in the other. She'd be wearing old slacks and a man's shirt and she'd look lovely.

"Damn you," she said suddenly.

"Why?"

"Because you wouldn't call at this hour just to be nice. I'm never awake this early and you know it. You've got some more detecting for me to do."

61

"I'm afraid you're right."

"Damn you again. What is it?"

"Clay."

"Clay," she said. "You want more inside info on this off-Broadway behemoth. You want the high-up way-out lowdown on this murky man of mystery, this heavy-weight hotster, this——"

"You should be ghosting for Winchell."

"I'm a gal of many talents," she said. "What do you want to know about him?"

"Who he is."

"Oh," she said heavily. "It couldn't be something simple, like what he eats for breakfast or what brand of cigarettes he smokes. Cigars, I mean. It has to be——"

"Just who he is. All I've got now is a name. I'd like a first name to go with it. If you can find out."

"Lee Brougham would know," she said thoughtfully. "But he's supposed to be in California. I told you that."

"Uh-huh."

She was silent for a miute. "This," she said, "is going to be a bitch."

"I'm afraid you're right."

"Hell of a conversation. You keep being afraid and I keep being right. Let me think this out for a minute, Ed. I can find out who directed 'Hungry Wedding.' Nobody would boast about it, but somebody must have directed the dog, and I can find out who. And he just might have a list of backers, which he just might let me look at. And Clay just might be on it. There's no guarantee, Ed. It's a shot in the dark."

"That's the only kind there is."

"So I'll fire away. It may take an hour and it may take six hours and it may take three weeks. Anything inter-esting happen last night?"

"Nothing much," I lied. "I spent a little time with a girl."

"Who?"

"You," I said. "Remember?"

"Ed——"

"I'll have more to tell you," I said. "When you get over here."

"Where?"

"Here," I said.

"Your apartment? No, don't tell me you're afraid again and I'm right again. You don't want me to call with the precious information. You want me to trot it over. Right?"

"Right."

She sighed. "I'll take cabs all over the city," she told me. "And I have a hunch you're going to wind up shelling out for another dinner tonight, Mr. London, sir."

"It's all deductible," I said. "See what you can find out."

I was lighting my pipe when the dorbell rang.

An hour had passed since I talked to Maddy. Maybe a little more than an hour—it was hard to say. I finished lighting the pipe and started for the door, then stopped when I was halfway there.

It was too soon for it to be Maddy. It could have been anybody else in the world, ranging from the Con Ed man coming to read my meter to a girl scout selling cookies. But I was feeling nervous. I went back for Armin's Beretta and hoped to God it wasn't a girl scout selling cookies.

I felt only halfway ridiculous holding the gun in one hand while I opened the door.

I felt completely ridiculous when the big one knocked it out of my hand.

There were two of them—a big one and a small one. The big one was very big, a little taller than I am and a hell of a lot wider. He had a boxer's flattened nose and a cretin idiot's fixed stare. His jacket was stretched tight across huge shoulders. His eyes were small and beady and his forehead was wide and dull.

The small one wasn't really that small—he looked small because he was standing next to a human mountain. He wore a hat and a suit and a tie. He had his hands in his pants pockets and he was smiling.

"Inside," he said. "Move."

I didn't move. The big one gave me a shove, his arm hardly moving, and I moved. I backed up fast and damn near fell over. The big one reached out a paw and scooped

63

up the Beretta. He pitched it at a chair. He seemed contemptuous of it, as if it was some kind of silly toy.

The small one turned, closed the door, slid the bolt across. He turned again, his eyes showing the same contempt for me that the big one had shown for the gun.

"Now," he said, "we talk. That briefcase."

SEVEN

THE big one held his hands in front of his chest and flexed his fingers. The small one had a bulge under his jacket that was either a gun or a lonely left breast. I remembered Peter Armin and thought about reasonable men. These two didn't look reasonable at all.

They didn't talk now. They were waiting me out, waiting for me to say something or do something. I wondered if I was supposed to offer them a drink.

"You're out in left field," I said finally. "I don't have the briefcase."

"The boss said you'd say that."

"It's the truth."

Their faces told me nothing. "The boss said to ask you nice," the smaller one said. "He said ask you nice, and if you didn't come up with the briefcase, then work you over."

"He had to send two of you?"

They didn't get angry. "Two of us," the talker said. "One to ask nice, the other to work you over. I'm asking nice. Billy takes care of the rest."

"I don't have the briefcase."

The little one considered that. He pursed his lips, narrowed his eyes, then made a small clucking sound with his tongue. "Billy," he said softly, "hit him."

Billy hit me in the stomach.

He wound up like a bush-league pitcher and telegraphed the punch all over the place. He had all the subtlety of a pneumatic hammer and I was too dumb to get out of the way. My legs turned to gelatin and I wound up on the floor. I opened my eyes, saw little black circles. I blinked the circles away and looked at Billy. His hands were in front of his chest again. He flexed them, smiling the smile of a competent workman who is proud of his craft.

Something made me get up. I wobbled around and wondered if he was going to hit me again. He didn't. I looked at him and watched his smile spread. I said a few words about Billy, and a few more about his mother, and still more about the probable relationship between the two of them.

He couldn't help understanding them. They were all about four letters long. He growled and moved at me.

"Billy!"

He grunted, stopped in his tracks. The hands that were balled into fist now unwound. He flexed his fingers.

"Don't get mad, Billy," the little one said.

"Aw, Ralph——"

"Don't get mad. You know what happens when you get mad. You blow up, you hit too hard, you hurt somebody more than you should. You know what the boss said. You do that again, you go out on your ear."

"He can't call me that kind of thing."

Ralph shrugged. "So his manners stink. It's not like he was saying the truth. Your mother's a wonderful woman."

"I love her."

"Of course you do," Ralph said. "Don't worry what this schmuck says. Forget about it."

He turned to me again. His tone was conversational. "Don't talk to Billy like that, London. He's an ex-pug. In the ring when he heard somebody call him a name, he went off his nut. Lost his control every time, swinging like a maniac. When he connected he won a lot of fights. Sometimes he missed. You he wouldn't miss, so don't talk dirty to him."

I didn't say anything.

"You remember where that briefcase is?"

"I told you——"

"We got orders, London. Don't try to sell us anything. Just give us the case."

"And if I don't? Are you going to beat me to death?"

He shook his head. "We search the place. The boss figures if you got the stuff it's not here anyhow, but we

66

look to make sure. Then we work you over so you know better. Just a light going-over. Not enough to put you in the hospital or anything. Just enough so next time the boss asks a favor you jump."

They were a pair of fairly complex machines, primed to do a task and nothing more. Reasoning with them was like reasoning with IBM's latest product. It couldn't work.

"You could save yourself a beating," Ralph said confidentially. "Billy works you over, it don't kill you but it don't do you any good either. It's the same either way. You lose the briefcase whether you get hit or not. And the next hit might be in the head. The boss doesn't like to hit people in the head if he can help it. Sometimes he can't help it."

I opened my mouth to tell him again that I didn't have the damned thing. I changed my mind before the sentence got going. I was starting to feel like a broken record.

Ralph shrugged at me again. "You're calling the shots," he said. "You change your mind while Billy's taking you apart, you tell me. He'll stop if I tell him to. And I'll tell him to when you cough up the briefcase." He turned his head slightly in Billy's direction. "Now take it easy on him, Billy. Go gentle. But let him feel it a little."

Billy heard the command and answered it like an old pug answering the bell. He moved toward me and all I could think was, dammit, this son of a bitch isn't going to hit me again. I stepped right at him and threw a right at his jaw.

He picked it off with his left, brushed it away like a cow's tail brushing flies.

Then he hit me in the stomach.

I didn't even have time to think about it. I went straight to my knees and used both hands to hold my guts together. This time I didn't try to get up. Billy helped me. He lifted me with one hand on my shirt front, hit me with the other hand, and I went down again.

"Prop him against the wall," Ralph suggested. "So he don't keep falling down. And pull the punches a little more. You're hitting a little too hard."

"I ain't hitting that hard, Ralph."

"A little easier," Ralph said. "His stomach's soft. He can't take too much punishment."

Billy picked me up again and stood me up against one wall. He hit me three more times. He was supposed to be letting up on the punches. Maybe he was. I couldn't tell.

My stomach was on fire. When I opened my eyes the room rocked like teen-ager's music. When I closed them it didn't help at all. He held me with one paw and slugged me with the other and I stood there like a sap and took it.

Ralph said: "Hold it."

Billy let go of me and I started to slide down the wall. It was a scene out of a Chaplin movie with the humor left on the cutting-room floor. He caught me easily and propped me up again.

"You had enough, London? You want to open up?"

I told him to go to hell.

"A hero," Ralph said.

I wasn't being a hero. I would have given him a brief-case full of H-bomb secrets without giving a damn at that point. But I didn't have it to give.

"Slap the hero, Billy. First take off your ring. We aren't supposed to mark him up."

Billy took a large signet ring from the third finger of his right hand. Then he held onto me with his left hand and started slapping me with the right one. He slapped forehand, then backhand, and between my head bounced off the wall. There was a regular pattern to it: slap, bump, slap, bump——

The pain stopped after a little while. I stopped feeling things, stopped seeing and stopped hearing. There was the blue-gray monotony of the slap bump slap bump, a deading rhythm that went on forever.

A voice came through a filter. "——just won't talk," it said. Then a few words were lost. Then: "——search the place. Won't find anything but the boss said take a look. Dump the schmuck and we'll look."

I wondered what "dump the schmuck" was supposed to mean. I opened my eyes and watched Billy cock a fist as big as a cannon ball. Then the fist exploded against my jaw and the universe went from gray to black.

It wasn't like waking up. The world came back into
focus a little at a time, a broken series of short gray
spasms in a world of black. A batch of disconnected
scenes, vague and partially formed, breaking up long
stretches of nothing in particular.

Someone talking in a low voice. The darkness again.

The phone ringing. I wanted to get up to answer it.
Instead I stayed where I was and counted the rings. I
kept losing count and starting over. Finally it stopped, or
I didn't hear it any more. Then the black curtain fell and
I was out again.

And then, very suddenly, I was awake.

I was lying on the floor against one wall—the wall Billy
had used to prop me up against. My head ached dully
and my jaw ached sharply and my stomach had a hole
in it. The hole was about the size of a large human fist.
It took me two tries to get to my feet. I staggered into
the bathroom and poured my stomach out. Then I took
four aspirins from the bottle in the medicine chest, carried
them back to the living room, washed them down with
a glassful of cognac.

The cognac was more important than the aspirins. The
aspirins took a minimum of two seconds to dissolve,
according to the ads. The cognac went to work instantly
to relieve aches and pains caused by headache, neuritis
and neuralgia.

It helped. My eyes focussed again and my knees
worked and I didn't notice my stomach as much as before. I took another belt from the bottle.

Then I saw what they had done to the apartment.

It didn't look as though a cyclone had hit it. A cyclone
isn't selective. It hits a whole area and knocks the hell
out of anything that gets in the way. They had been more
selective.

But just as destructive.

The Bokhara was rolled up in one corner of the room
and the floor was bare. But even with the rug rolled up
you couldn't see too much of the floor. It was covered
with things.

It was covered with every book that had been in the bookcases. Maybe the bastards thought I hid the brief-case behind the books. Maybe they were just being thorough. I looked down at a collection of Stephen Crane first editions, picked up a copy of 'The Little Regiment.' The spine was broken.

The cushions of the two leather chairs leaked their stuffing onto the floor. Ralph—or Billy, it didn't matter which one—had slashed them open with a knife. Two reproductions lay curling at the edges. The Miro had a footprint in the middle and the Tanguy was in shreds. They had been ripped from their frames.

I found a pack of cigarettes and got one going. There was more, plenty more, but I didn't feel like looking at it. I went to the bedroom and sat down on the edge of the bed. That room was a mess, too, but not quite as bad.

And the damnedest thing was that I knew they hadn't ruined anything on purpose. They weren't trying to do damage any more than they were trying to prevent it. They were machines, with a single job to do, and every-thing else was incidental. They were supposed to beat me up—not kill me, not send me to the hospital.

And they did just that. I was on my feet already, with nothing to show for it but a pain in the gut and an aching head. The headache would be gone in the morning, the rest wouldn't last much longer.

I ground out the cigarette. Who was I supposed to hate? Bannister, of course. He was the man who gave the order, the leading bastard who gave the order that sent the two minor bastards on my neck. He killed a blonde and had the crap knocked out of a private detec-tive and he was going to get his.

And Ralph and Billy. Now how the hell could I hate Billy? He was a mongoloid with muscles and he prac-ticed the only trade he knew. When he was a fighter he got paid for beating other fighters senseless. Now he did the same work without ropes or gloves. Do you hate a machine?

Or Ralph. He was a company man to the core, a junior executive, and he'd be the same guy underneath if he worked for General Motors or Jimmy Hoffa or the CIA.

70

He even tried his best to save me from a beating. Hate him?

I didn't hate them, didn't hate Ralph and didn't hate Billy. They weren't the kind of people you hated.

But I was in their debt and I'm the kind of slob who likes to mark his debts paid. I owed them for a beating and a wrecked apartment. It was a debt I was going to pay.

I was going to kill them.

I went back to the living room and looked at wreckage for a few long minutes. A little of that goes a long way. I picked up the telephone and called a girl named Cora Johnson. She's a girl in her middle twenties, a very bright gal with a degree from City College. She is also a Negro, and she earns a small living doing housework. They do things strangely in the United States some of the time.

I asked her if she could come over in an hour or two and she said she could. I told her the place looked like hell with a hangover, that she should do whatever she could and not worry about it. "Just set the books in the bookcases," I told her. "I can rearrange them later. Try to make the place livable again. I'll leave a key under the mat for you."

She didn't ask what had happened. I knew she wouldn't ask, and that she'd keep her mouth shut. She was that sort of person.

I was still standing around, wondering where to go next and who to see next, when the bell rang. The doorbell.

And I knew right away who it was. Ralph and Billy, coming back to give me another spin through the old slap bump circuit, another chance to be a good little boy and give them a briefcase that I didn't have.

This time it was going to be different.

I must have been a little bit insane. I found the Beretta on the floor—they hadn't even bothered to take it with them. I picked it up and curled my index finger around the trigger. I walked to the door and stood there with my hand on the knob, ready to give the trigger a squeeze the minute I saw them. Billy wasn't going to knock the gun out of my hand this time, by George. I'd shoot him first.

71

I turned the knob. I gave the door a yank and stuck the gun in my visitor's face.

And Maddy Parson let out a small scream.

It took a few minutes to calm her down. "You were joking," she said uncertainly. "It was your idea of a gag. Well, it wasn't very funny. I could have had a heart attack. Is that thing loaded, Ed?"

"I hope so."

"You———"

"Come on inside," I said. "Relax. Everything's all right."

She took a few steps inside, got a good look at the apartment, and let go of her jaw. It fell three inches. "Okay," she said. "What happened?"

"I dropped my watch."

"A cyclone hit it. Now open up, Ed. All of it."

I didn't tell her the difference between Billy and Ralph and a cyclone. She would have missed the point. It was easier to sit her down and explain the whole thing as quickly as I could, from Armin through Billy and Ralph. I left out the names and the descriptions but that was all I left out. By the time I was done she had a face the color of ashes.

She said: "Oh, Holy Christ. They could have killed you."

"Not in a million years."

"But———"

"Look at me," I said. "I didn't even get a bloody nose. Not even a sprained thumb. And right this minute I'm so full of cognac I can't feel a damned thing. I'll sit around aching tomorrow, maybe. And the day after that it'll hurt once in a while. And nothing the day after that one. Nothing resembling a permanent injury. Those two are professionals, Maddy."

"They're animals."

"Then they're professional animals. An amateur could have killed me by accident, would have cracked a rib or two, anyway. But they were perfect. They knew just what to do and they did it."

72

She shuddered. I put an arm around her and she turned to me and hugged me. I saw a drop of wet saltiness running down one cheek, wiped it up with a finger.

"Hell, you were right." She looked at me. "When you said you could cry on cue," I explained.

She looked away. "Just shut up," she said. "Or I'll hit you in the stomach. At least I get a chance to play nurse. You're going to bed now, Ed."

"Like hell I am."

"Ed——"

"I couldn't fall asleep if I wanted to. And I don't want to. Things are coming to a head, Maddy. A whole slew of two-legged bombs are running around waiting to go off."

"And you want to be blown up?"

"I want to be there. I want to watch the explosion, set off a bomb or two of my own."

"You should go right to sleep."

I shook my head, which was a mistake. It ached. "I wouldn't stay here anyway. I was letting them come to me, Maddy. It made sense before. Now I'd rather be a moving target. I have to start things on my own."

"Then go to a hotel. In the morning——"

"The morning's too late."

She sighed. It was a long and very female sigh. She really wanted to put me to bed and tuck me in and listen to my prayers. The mother instinct dies hard.

"All right," she said sadly. "Where are you going to start?"

"Probably with Armin."

"Armin?"

"The little man who was waiting for me last night. Mr. Neatness and Light. His name's Peter Armin and he's staying at a midtown hotel. I think he'll be glad to see me."

"Why him?"

"Because I know where he is. Because I know who he is, as far as that goes. And because I think he'll help me."

"Why should he?"

I stood up. "Because I may be able to help him," I

73

said. "Say, you didn't come up with anything, did you? About Clay?"

She looked stunned. She made a small fist out of one hand and used it to tap herself on the jaw. Then she sat there shaking her head from side to side at me.

"I completely forgot," she said. "God, I'm stupid. How can I be so stupid? I was so busy listening to you and all that I forgot all about it."

"All about what?"

"It's probably nothing," she said. "I chased all over town looking for that director, Ed, and I couldn't find him. Nobody knew just where he was. He's a periodic drunk or something and he was missing his period. Or having it."

I waited for her to get to the point. If I knew who Clay was, I didn't necessarily have to bother with Armin. Because Clay was the boy I needed, the missing factor in the equation.

He had the briefcase.

"So I couldn't find him," she was saying. "But I got hold of another guy, one who collects lists of angels so hard-up producers can hunt up soft touches. He had the list for 'Hungry Wedding'!"

"And Clay was on it?"

"I don't know."

"Huh?"

"There was no Mr. Clay," she said. "But then I got the bright idea that Clay could be a first name instead of a last name. So I went through the list again and found a man named Clayton. That's his first name. They didn't have his address."

I let out a lot of breath. "That has to be him. What was his last name?"

"Just a minute. It's on the tip of my tongue, Ed. It was something like Rail but that wasn't it. Kale? Crail? Oh, damn it to hell——"

"Maddy——"

"Oh, it's nothing to worry about. I wrote it down, for Pete's sake. I'm just so darn mad that I couldn't remember it. Just a minute—it's somewhere in my purse."

I waited while she rummaged through a purse and kept

saying darn it. Then she managed to find her wallet, took it out and managed to find a slip of paper. She looked at it and smiled proudly at me.

"This is the one," she said, very positively. "No address, just the name."

I told her to read it.

"Clayton Bannister," she read calmly. "Does that mean anything?"

EIGHT

THE human equation picked itself up, dusted itself off and crawled furtively into the woodwork. I wanted to get down on all fours and crawl after it. Everything had worked out so neatly, so flawlessly. Bannister and Armin wanted the briefcase and Clay had the briefcase and——

Sure they did, London.

I told Maddy all about it and watched her eyes bulge. Two suspects had turned into one, with Clay and Bannister the two sides of the same damn coin.

"Then," she wanted to know, "who has the briefcase?"

Briefcase, briefcase, who's got the briefcase. "It's a good question," I told her. "We'll have to find out. Now."

I grabbed a jacket and a hat and we got out of the apartment. I locked the door and pitched a key under the mat for Cora. Then we left the building.

She wanted me to buy her dinner but I managed to talk her out of the idea of a real meal. Instead we found a deli with a pair of formica-topped tables in the rear. A moon-faced man with bushy eyebrows brought us pastrami sandwiches on fresh rye and two bottles of cold Dutch beer. The apron covering his beer belly was spotless, probably because he didn't wipe his dirty hands on it.

Every once in a while an indefatigable cockroach scurried across the floor at our feet. Even this couldn't spoil our appetites. We wolfed down the sandwiches and swilled beer and got out of there.

"Now I put you in a cab and send you home," I said optimistically.

She wasn't having any. "I'm going with you, Ed."

"Don't be——"

"Silly? I'm not being silly."

"I wasn't going to say that."

"Oh? What were you going to say?"

"I was going to say Don't be ridiculous."

"Darn it, Ed——"

"One of two things could happen or both," I told her. "You could get hurt or you could get in the way. I don't want either one. Therefore——"

"There's another alternative, Ed. I could be of help. To tell the truth, I don't see how you get along without me. You may be a brilliant detective but you forget the elementary things."

"Like what?"

"Like Clayton Bannister," she said. "God, you didn't even look him up in the phone book. You know his full name and you leave it alone."

"He won't be listed."

"Are you sure? So sure you won't take the trouble to look?"

Arguing with Maddy was like swimming in a vat of mercury. There was no future in it. We ducked into a drugstore and I went through the Manhattan and Bronx books, the only ones on hand. There were twenty-one Bannisters in Manhattan and nine in the Bronx and none of them was named Clayton. One guy was listed as C Bannister and Maddy wanted me to call him. I told her he lived on Essex Street and our boy wasn't going to turn up in a Lower East Side slum.

So she made me call Information and check on the possibility of a Clayton Bannister in Brooklyn or Queens. The operator was a good sport. She checked. No Clayton Bannister in Brooklyn, none in Queens. Not even one on Staten Island.

So I won the battle and lost the war. I couldn't get rid of Maddy. She had to come along, had to help me find Armin.

We used the drugstore's back door in case one of Bannister's little men was doing a shadow job. We wound up in an alley, followed it to the nearest street and caught the first cab that came by. We hopped into the back seat and I felt like the all-American folk hero, with an arm around Maddy, a hand on the Beretta in my pocket. All I needed was a hip flask.

I had an insane urge to shout FOLLOW THAT CAR! at our driver. But there was no car in front of us. So that killed that.

The Ruskin was a throwback to better times. It stood twelve stories tall at the corner of Eighth Avenue and Forty-fourth Street and remembered the days when the West Side was the best side, which was a long time ago. Now Broadway was fast-buck alley and Eighth Avenue was Whore Row.

The Ruskin stared across early-evening Eighth Avenue, watching whores bloom in doorways like pretty weeds in a dying garden. The lobby was filled with overstuffed Edwardian chairs. The ceiling was high and dripped with chandeliers. We walked to the front desk while thirty or forty years seem to slip away and disappear.

I watched expressions play across the face of the middle-aged desk clerk. Maddy and I weren't married— she wasn't wearing a ring. And we weren't toting luggage. But it was damned early for adultery, wasn't it? And we didn't look like whore and customer.

He just about had his mind made up to take a chance on us when we disappointed him. I told him I wanted to talk to Room 1104 on the house phone. He did a very sad double take, then pointed to a phone on the desk and scuttled for the switchboard. Midway through the first ring Peter Armin picked up the phone and said hello to me.

"Ed London," I said. "Can I come up?"

A small and brief sigh came over the wire. "I am delighted," he said. "I'll be most happy to see you. Where are you?"

"In the lobby."

He chuckled appreciatively. "Magnificent," he said. "You give little advance warning, Mr. London. Would you wait five minutes or so, then come straight up?"

I told him that was fine, put the phone down. I asked the clerk at the desk if the hotel had a bar. He pointed through a wide doorway and I took Maddy by the arm and led her toward it.

"I don't want a drink," she said. "Why don't we stay in the lobby?"

"Because Bannister may have the place watched. Maybe his man missed us on the way in. If we sit around the lobby he's sure to spot us."

"That makes sense."

"No, it doesn't," I told her. "But I need a drink."

The bar matched the lobby. It was more along the lines of an old-style taproom than a hotel bar. I asked for Courvoisier and while the barman poured my drink Maddy changed her mind and ordered a Daiquiri.

"I thought you weren't having any."

"I wasn't," she said. "Ed, I'm worried."

"I told you to go home."

She shook her head impatiently. "I'd worry even more if you were here without me. Look, how do you know what we're walking into? He could have a trap for us."

"Trap? Hell, all he'll do is sit there with a gun in his hand. He'll do that just as a matter of course to make sure I'm not here with Bannister at my heels. But he won't try to trap me. He trapped me before in my own apartment, for God's sake. He doesn't want me. He wants the briefcase."

"So does Bannister. And look what his men did to you."

I told her Bannister and Armin were different men. Their minds worked differently.

She picked up her glass, finished most of it in one swallow. "What are you going to say to him?"

"That we should cooperate."

"Huh?"

"He wants a breifcase," I said. "I want a killer. That doesn't mean we have to fight each other. I've got a hunch he's in a spot like mine. I think he must be working alone. He could probably use somebody on his side."

"And you'll be on his side?"

I couldn't tell whether she approved or disapproved. She read the line perfectly straight.

I sipped cognac. I said: "I'm not sure. I'll have to see

79

how it goes upstairs. If nothing else, we can probably pool information. He must know the answers to a hell of a lot of questions."

"Like what?"

"Like what's in the briefcase and what's so important about it. Like why the girl was killed and where she fits into the picture. I'm in the middle of everything and I don't know what it's all about, Maddy. Armin can be of help."

"If he wants to."

"Well, sure," I said. "If he wants to."

We left the elevator and found Room 1104 without a hell of a lot of trouble. I knocked on the door and Armin's voice told us to come in.

He was sitting in a chair with a gun in his hand. Every time I saw him he was sitting with a gun in his hand. This one was a Beretta like the first. It was the mate to the one in my pocket.

"This is getting monotonous," I said. He lowered the gun and Maddy relaxed her grip on my arm.

"I'm terribly sorry," Peter Armin said. "You understand, of course. I didn't know for certain that you'd be alone. But that's impolite, isn't it? You're not alone. I don't believe I've met the young lady."

"My secretary."

He nodded with majestic understanding. He was dressed well, almost too well. He wore a pair of light-gray flannel slacks and a lime-green Paisley shirt with a button-down collar. The shirt was open at the neck. He wasn't wearing a tie. His shoes and socks were black.

"This room is really too small," he said. "Only the one chair. If you'd care to sit on the bed—"

We sat on the bed.

"I'm glad you came in person," he went on. "I was afraid you might wish to talk on the phone. I really cannot do business over the telephone. The personal element is lost."

He killed a little time finding his pack of cigarettes and offering them around. We thanked him and passed them up. He lit a cigarette for himself, smoked thoughtfully.

80

"You've decided to sell me the briefcase, Mr. London?"

I killed time on my own by filling a pipe and lighting it. Maddy got a cigarette and I lit it for her. The three of us sat and smoked.

Finally I said: "You're a reasonable man, Armin."

"I try to be."

"Then let me set up a logical argument. Will you hear me out?"

"With pleasure."

"Good," I said. "Now let's postulate that I don't have the briefcase, don't know much about it. Can you accept that?"

"As a postulate."

"Good. Bannister's men paid me a visit this afternoon. They came to my apartment. There were two of them. A talker named Ralph and a gorilla named Billy."

"I was afraid that would happen," he said ruefully. "I tried to warn you, Mr. London."

"Sure, but I didn't have the briefcase. Don't forget that postulate we're working on."

"I see."

I drew on my pipe and blew out smoke. "The way I see it, you and Bannister are on opposite sides of the fence."

"Precisely. And it's a high fence, Mr. London."

"You and I are reasonable men. Bannister is not. If I have to take sides, your side is the natural one to pick."

He nodded with obvious approval. "That only stands to reason," he said. "As you may remember, it was my whole point in our . . . conference last evening. A choice of mind over muscle, one might almost say."

"Uh-huh." I looked at him. "So where are we? You and I are natural allies. Bannister's our natural enemy. You want to get hold of a briefcase. I want to get Bannister for murder—Alicia Arden's murder."

He nodded.

"The briefcase is worth ten grand to you——"

"More, really. But I can only pay ten thousand."

"So call it ten thousand. And nailing Bannister to an electric chair is worth a lot of time and effort to me."

"A worthy aim, Mr. London."

I smiled. It was easy to like Armin. You can't hate a man who speaks your own language, can't despise a guy whose mind works the way your own mind works. Every time he opened his mouth I liked him a little bit more.

"What I'm proposing," I said, "is a sort of holy alliance."

"Against Bannister?"

"Uh-huh."

"Go on," he said. "Your proposition sounds appealing."

"We work together," I said. "We pool information—you've probably got more to contribute than I do—and we join forces. You help me pin down Bannister and I help you get the briefcase. If I get my hands on it I give it to you for five thousand dollars—half of what it's worth to you. If you get it alone, it's yours free and clear."

He stubbed out his cigarette very elaborately in a small glass ashtray. "I'd pay you the five thousand in any event," he said slowly. "I really would prefer it that way. Otherwise you'd have reason to work at cross-purposes with me under certain circumstances. If either of us recovers the briefcase, you'll still get five thousand dollars."

I said that was fine.

He thought some more. "One thing disturbs me, Mr. London. How can you be certain that I won't run off and leave you to chase Mr. Bannister alone once I've got the briefcase? Or that I'll pay you for it?"

"I can't."

He turned both palms upward. His gun was tucked into the arm of the chair. "Then——"

"By the same token," I said, "how can you be sure I won't let you go to hell once I get Bannister? We're both taking a chance, Armin. I don't mind trusting you. I think you're trustworthy."

He laughed, delighted. "Perhaps I am," he admitted. "Up to a point. Do you know something? I really believe now that you don't have that briefcase, Mr. London. And that you never did have it at all."

"I told you that before."

"But I didn't believe you before."

"And you believe me now?"

He produced his pack of Turkish cigarettes again, offered them around again, lit one again for himself. "Do you know anything about confidence men, Mr. London?"

"A little."

"I've had some experience in that area," he said confidentially. "One does so many things in order to survive. Are you familiar with the First Law of Con?"

I wasn't.

"Very simply: If the mark does not see your point of profit, you may sell him real estate on the planet Jupiter. If, so far as he can see, there's no reason for you to be swindling him, you can steal him blind."

"Uh-huh."

He smiled pleasantly. "So," he said. "For a moment let's take a different postulate. Let us assume that you do indeed possess the briefcase. If so, what possible advantage could you hope to gain by this meeting tonight? You want to get five thousand for the case when I've already offered you ten. I have to assume you're telling the truth, Mr. London. Otherwise I can't see your point of profit."

Maddy was grinning. She had come to Armin's room determined to hate the little man. Now she liked him. He was a charming son of a bitch.

"I accept your terms," he said. "One hand shall wash the other, as it were. It is a bargain."

I hesitated.

"Isn't it a bargain?"

"Just one thing," I said. "About the briefcase."

"Go on."

"If it contains espionage material, it's no bargain. Papers relating to the security of the United States of America . . . Hell, you know the cliché, I'm sure."

He smiled.

"I'm an American," I went on. "I don't wave the flag, don't sit around telling everybody what a goddam patriot I am. But I don't play traitor either."

He puffed on his cigarette. "I understand," he said. "I was not born in this country myself, as you must have guessed. My native land doesn't exist at the present time.

83

It was a small state in the Balkans. The patchwork quilt of Europe—that's what they once called it. Now the patchwork quilt has turned into a red carpet. But that doesn't matter.

"I've travelled all over the world, Mr. London. You might call me a picaresque character. I've lived by my wits, really. Now I live in the United States. I married an America girl, and, a number of years ago became a naturalized citizen."

He smiled at the memory. "I prefer this country," he said. "However, I don't think it's paradise on earth, or that all other countries are perforce wretched and abominable. I've been to them and I know better. The fact that you elect your officials and that these elections, except in certain urban localities, are honest ones, doesn't intrigue me much. I'm a selfish man, Mr. London. In the pure sense of the word. My comfort is more important to me than abstract justice."

"That's not so uncommon."

"Probably not. But what I'm really trying to say is that I find it easier and more pleasant to live in America. The police may not be honest, but they are a little less blatant in their thievery. They may slap a person around but rarely beat him to death. A person's more free to live his own life here."

He sighed. "I won't go so far as to say that I wouldn't sell out the United States of America. I know myself too well. I probably would. But the price would be extremely high."

The room stayed silent for several seconds then. I glanced at Maddy. She'd been listening very carefully to Armin and her face was thoughtful. I looked back at Armin. He was putting out his cigarette. I wondered if he had meant to say all that he said, if maybe his words had carried him away.

He looked up, his eyes bright. "I become intolerably long-winded at times," he said apologetically. "You asked a most simple question and I delivered myself of a long sermon which didn't even supply the answer to your question. Set your mind at rest, Mr. London. I'm no spy. The briefcase contains no State secrets."

"That's good."

"Thus," he said, "there are no problems, no barriers between us. Unless you have another question?"

"That's all."

"Then we work together? It's a bargain?"

"It's a bargain," I said.

NINE

HE shook out a cigarette and held it loose and limp between the thumb and forefinger of his right hand. He didn't light it. Instead he turned it over and over, staring thoughtfully at it. Suddenly he shrugged and stuck it back in the pack.

"I smoke too much," he said. "I also have a tendency to waste a great deal of time. But it is difficult to know where to begin. I want to give you as much information as I possibly can, yet I also want to take up a minimum of your time. Your time and mine as well. Time is precious. We will profit more through action than through words. Yet words are essential, too."

In turn he studied the floor and the ceiling and his neatly manicured fingernails. He looked up at me. "Let me begin somewhere in the neighborhood of the beginning, Mr. London. You are a detective. Your profession must bring you in line with crime and criminals to a greater or lesser degree. Perhaps you've heard of the Wallstein jewels?"

A soft bell rang somewhere in the back of my mind. I told him I never heard of the jewels.

He said: "Franz Wallstein was the second son of a Prussian industrialist. He was born shortly after the turn of the century. His father was a typical member of the Junker caste—a second or third-rate Krupp or Thiessen. The older son—I believe his name was Reinhardt, not that it matters—followed the father into the firm. Franz, the younger son, struck out on his own. In the early thirties he entered the service of a particularly noxious Austrian corporal."

"Hitler."

"Or Schicklgruber, as you prefer it. Franz Wallstein was neither well-mannered nor intelligent. Followers of fascist movements rarely are. His sole virtue was his dedication to this questionable cause. While never becoming particularly important, he rose to his own level quickly and enjoyed a certain amount of security. He possessed the qualifications of height, blonde hair, blue eyes. He was assigned to a troop of Himmler's Elite Guards in the SS. Later, during the war, he was placed second in command at one of the larger concentration camps. I think it was Belsen; I'm not entirely sure. In that capacity his dedication did not prove entirely flawless. He stole."

I lit my pipe. "You were talking about jewels."

"That's correct," he said, but went on as though he hadn't been interrupted. "It was standard operating procedure to confiscate any and all possessions of concentration camp prisoners, up to and including the gold from their teeth after they had been gassed. This property, in theory, became the property of the German Reich, but the facts did not always follow theory. Goering, for example, looted Europe to augment his private art collection. Minor guards would take wrist watches for themselves, a bracelet for a wife or mistress. Franz Wallstein followed along these lines. He seemed to have an interest in precious stones. If a prisoner managed to retain possession of valuable jewelry until he reached Wallstein's camp, the jewels generally wound up in Wallstein's footlocker."

He stood up, paused for breath. "Things went smoothly for Wallstein," he went on. "They did not go smoothly for Nazi Germany. The war moved to an end. Wallstein was at once a hunted man, no longer a trusted servant of a secure government. He was not pursued as avidly as Bormann or Eichmann or Himmler himself. But he was on the wanted lists, as they say. His wife was pregnant at the time and must have seemed like excess baggage to him. He left her in Germany, bundled up his jewels and fled the country.

"He went first to Mexico. The political climate there soon turned out to be less than ideal and within several months it was time for him to make his move again. This time he picked a nation where he felt he would be more welcome. He chose Argentina."

I shook out my pipe, glanced briefly at Maddy. She was listening closely. So was I, but I wished he would get to the point already. Bannister and the briefcase were more important to me than a crooked Nazi and stolen jewels.

"Argentina was a natural home for him," Armin went on. "It is certain that he found countrymen there. German is supposed to be the second language of Buenos Aires. Wallstein made himself comfortable, bought an attractive house in a fashionable suburb and married a local girl without bothering to divorce the wife he'd left in Germany. He changed his name to Heinz Linder and opened an importing concern in Buenos Aires. Strong rumor has it that he engaged in smuggling of one sort or another, probably of narcotics. But this remains to be proved. Q.E.D. Whatever his actual means of support, Wallstein-Linder added to his collection of jewels. They reposed in a wall safe on the second floor of his home."

"And somebody hit the safe?"

He sighed. "Not exactly, Mr. London. The situation is a bit more complex than that. Wallstein was not entirely forgotten. A group of Israeli agents similar to the ones who caught Eichmann were looking for former SS men, Wallstein among them. Two agents followed his trail to Mexico City and lost him there. A few years later they extended the trail to Buenos Aires."

The bell went off again, louder this time. "I remember now," I said. "About a year ago. He was found dead in Argentina and identified as Wallstein. There was a short article in the *Times*."

Armin was nodding, smiling. "The same man," he said. "There wasn't much of a story at the time. The Israelis didn't bother to drag him off for a trial as they did with Eichmann. Franz Wallstein was not that important. They only wished to even the score with him: they tracked him down, broke into his home, shot him dead and left him to rot. The news value was small. The Argentine officials denied that he was Wallstein, not wanting to be accused of harboring a fugitive. The Israelis leaked the story but it still got little publicity."

"They shot him and took the jewels?"

"No, of course not. They were assassins, not thieves. They did their work and left him there. But the small amount of publicity attendant upon the killing was enough to attract the attention of that sort of professional criminal who specializes in precious stones. A ring of Canadian jewel thieves flew down to Buenos Aires and stole the jewels. I don't know the precise details of the crime but it was done well, it seems. They broke into Wallstein's home, tied up his widow, tied up her maid, cracked the safe, grabbed up the jewels and took the first plane out of the country. As I heard it, they were in and out of Argentina in less than twenty-four hours. That may be an exaggeration. At any rate, they worked quickly and left no traces."

"Any insurance?"

He chuckled. "On stolen jewels? Hardly. He was just a small-scale importer with not too much money—on the surface. He couldn't attract attention by insuring his collection. It was too great a risk."

I nodded. "Go on," I said.

He shook a cigarette from his pack again and rolled it around some more between his fingers. This time he put it to his lips and lighted it. He drew in smoke.

"Sorry," I said. "I didn't mean to change the subject."

"But you didn't, Mr. London."

"No?"

"Not at all. The fact that the jewels were not insured is really most relevant. Do you know much about jewel thieves?"

I didn't know a hell of a lot. "They're supposed to be an elite criminal class," I said. "They steal jewels and sell them to a fence. That's about all I know."

"They're elite," he said. "The rest is inaccurate."

He smiled when my eyebrows went up. "For a good group of jewel thieves, a fence is a last resort. Their first contact is with the insurance company."

I didn't get it.

"Let us suppose that a collection of gems is insured for half a million dollars, Mr. London. Once the theft is a *fait accompli* the company is legally obligated to pay out

89

the face value of the policy to the policyholder. Now let's suppose further that an agent for the thieves approaches an agent of the insurance company and offers to sell the jewels back for, say, two hundred thousand dollars. The company invariably pays. It's a clear saving to them of three hundred thousand. And a top thief always prefers to deal with an insurance company, you see. He gets a better price and runs less risk of a double cross."

"Why?"

"Because the company has to preserve its good name in criminal circles. I'm not joking, Mr. London. It sounds ludicrous at first but it follows the laws of logic. Perhaps, insurance companies only encourage criminal behavior by this practice. They don't seem to care. The figures on their own balance sheets are of greater concern to them."

"That's . . . that's unfair!"

That was Maddy talking and we both turned to look at her. Armin grinned at her. He said: "Unfair? To whom, my dear? Not to the policyholder, certainly—he gets his —possibly—irreplaceable jewelry returned. And not to the insurance company, which saves money. And not to the thieves, unfair to whom?"

"To the public——"

"Oh, but the public gains, too," Armin told her. "Any loss the company sustains is passed on to the public in the form of higher premiums, therefore, it's to the public's advantage for the company to save money."

"But—"

She stopped after the one word and looked around vacantly. She was very unhappy. She's slick and smooth and big-city, but she was lost now. I rescued her.

"Okay," I said. "The jewels weren't insured and the Canadians had troubles."

"Correct," he said. "They had troubles. They flew from Buenos Aires to New York, then from New York to Toronto. That was their base of operations. They cached the spoils and took up residence, for a time, in some hotels on Yonge Street."

"How many were there?"

"Four men."

"And how much were the jewels worth?"

"That's hard to say. Prices of stolen goods are almost incalculable, Mr. London. There are so many factors involved. The Hope Diamond is priceless, for example but worthless to a thief. He couldn't sell it."

I wanted facts and he kept giving me background. "That doesn't apply here," I told him. "The original owners are nameless, probably dead."

"Precisely. The Wallstein jewels are as readily convertible into cash as valuable jewels could be. Still, an appraisal is difficult. The figures I've heard quoted place the total worth at somewhere around four hundred thousand dollars. Retail, that is."

I whistled. Maddy took a deep breath. And Peter Armin smiled.

I said: "That's a lot of money."

"And that's an understatement. At any rate, the thieves had to find a fence, a receiver for the jewels. Two of them were in debt and strapped for cash. They couldn't unload a little at a time. They needed a big buyer to take the lot off their hands right away. They were willing to settle for one hundred thousand."

The picture was shaping up but the edges were still fuzzy. I wanted to hurry him up but it didn't seem possible. He was giving me plenty of theory and plenty of background with an occasional fact for flavor. He sat in his chair and smoked his Turkish cigarettes and I listened to him.

"The thieves knew several reliable fences. All of them were financially incapable of handling a transaction of such proportion. They might have arranged to split the deal between a few of them but they wanted to get it all over with in a hurry. They wanted one fence for the works." He paused for breath. "They couldn't find such a man in Toronto. There was one in New York, but they knew him solely by reputation."

"Bannister?"

"Of course. Mr. Clayton Bannister. What do you know about him, Mr. London?"

I knew that he played rough and talked ugly. I knew I didn't like him at all.

"Not much," I said.

"A most impressive man in his own way. He began during World War II with two partners named Ferber and Marti. The three of them grew fat with a number of black market operations. Gasoline stamps, unobtainable items, that sort of thing. They made a good thing of the war, Mr. London. Of the three, Mr. Bannister alone remains. Mr. Ferber and Mr. Marti are dead. Murdered."

"By Bannister?"

"Undoubtedly, but no one ever managed to prove it. Since then he's made an enormous amount of money in extra-legal activities while retaining a veneer of respectability. He has close ties with the local syndicate and remains independent at the same time. I've already said that he acts as a receiver of stolen goods. He does other things. He probably imports heroin, probably exports gold, probably receives smuggled diamonds and similar contraband. He heads a small but strong organization and his men are surprisingly loyal to him. He rewards the faithful and kills traitors. A good policy."

"What does he look like?"

"Like a gorilla. But I can do better than that. I have one of the few photographs in existence of him. A rare item, that. Here—have a look at it."

He took a snapshot from the pigskin pocket secretary and passed it to me. I looked at a head-and-shoulders shot of a man about forty with a massive and almost hairless head, a wide dome with fringe around the edges. He had a bulldog jaw and beady pig eyes set wide in a slab of a forehead. The mouth was a firm thin line, the nose regular, a little thick at the bridge.

I studied it, passed it to Maddy. "This the man at the party?"

She looked at it.

"Add five years," Armin told her. "Add twenty or thirty pounds. Add the foul-smelling cigar he habitually smokes. And you'll have Mr. Bannister."

She said: "I think it's him."

"But you're not sure?"

"Almost sure, Ed. He had a hat on when I saw him and he never took it off. And that bald head is the most distinctive feature in the picture. I'm trying to imagine him with a hat on. I didn't get a good look at him and it was months ago and there wasn't any point in remembering him, not at the time. But I'm pretty sure it's him."

"It has to be," I told her. I turned to Armin. "Okay—how did the thieves get in touch with him?"

"They didn't."

"No?"

"Not exactly," he said. He lit another cigarette and looked at me through a cloud of hazy smoke. "Mr. Bannister seemed to be the right man for them. But they didn't really trust him. None of them knew him. Honor among thieves is largely a romantic invention and they had no cause to believe that Mr. Banniser was an honorable man. They wanted to deal with him without getting close."

"Sure. They couldn't stop him from taking the jewels and telling them to go to hell."

"Precisely. They could hardly take him to court. They had skill and wits while he had muscle. They picked an intermediary, a go-between."

"And that's where you fit in?"

He laughed. "No, not I. Not at all. One of the thieves was sleeping with an American girl at the time. They sent her to New York with a message for Mr. Bannister."

Maddy said: "Sheila Kane."

"If you wish. They knew her as Alicia Arden. A young girl, young and strangely innocent. A lost soul, to be maudlin and poetic about it. Previously she had associated with elements of what they seem to call the Beat Generation. That was in San Francisco. In Los Angeles her friends were petty mobsters. By this time she was living with a jewel thief in Toronto. He briefed her, sent her to New York."

I tried to picture the girl. 'Young and strangely innocent.' A girl who ran with thieves and who found Jack Enright exciting, awe-inspiring. She made a funny picture. Every time I learned something new about her, the picture went out of focus and came back different.

"Now the plot thickens," Armin was saying. "A cliché. But an apt one. Alicia came to New York with a

93

few sample jewels and hunted for Mr. Bannister. He tries to pass himself off as a country squire. Has a large estate in Avalon on the tip of Long Island. He's a minor patron of the arts—supports a poor painter or two, donates regularly and substantially to several museums, occasionally backs a theatrical production. Alicia got his ear on one pretext or another, then told him her business."

"And he liked it?"

He sighed. "The details grow difficult now. Hazy. Mr. Bannister must have suggested a double cross—she would help him and they would leave the thieves out in the cold. Maybe he offered her twenty or thirty thousand outright. That must have looked better than whatever crumbs her boy friend was tossing her. At any rate, she cooperated with Mr. Bannister.

"She told the thieves to come to New York with the jewels. They let her know where they were staying and she relayed the information to Mr. Bannister. Then she went to their hiding place with one hundred thousand dollars. She paid them. They were supposed to give her the jewels in return. They didn't."

"You mean they were rigging a double cross of their own?"

He shook his head. "Not at all. Really, they were honest in their way. They feared Mr. Banniser and wanted to be out of the city before he could get to them. Instead of the jewels they gave Alicia the briefcase."

I said: "I thought we'd get to that sooner or later. Now what in hell is in the briefcase?"

"Directions. A set of directions and a pair of keys which would permit the holder of the case to claim the jewels. They thought this would save them from a cross, since Mr. Bannister couldn't chance killing them before he had the jewels. They were wrong."

"How?"

"Alicia traded the money for the briefcase and left. Minutes later Bannister's thugs broke in on the thieves and took back the money. The thieves disappeared."

"They skipped town?"

"I rather doubt it," he said. "I believe a cement over-

94

coat is the American term. You could probably find the four of them on the river bottom."

Maddy shuddered. I put an arm around her and Armin looked on with fatherly approval.

"It all grows jumbled after that point," he said. "I believe Alicia carried her double cross to its logical conclusion. She had the briefcase. It could make her richer than cooperation with Mr. Bannister could. So she stopped being Alicia Arden and turned into Sheila Kane. She must have been planning this all along. Her alias was established in advance."

"Maybe she was afraid of winding up in the river. Or maybe she wanted the twenty grand in her hands before she gave him the case."

Armin conceded that was possible. "She disappeared," he said. "Several weeks passed. Then everybody found the poor girl at once. Mr. Bannister found her and had her murdered. But he didn't recover the briefcase. You found her, but you didn't find the case either. I was certain you had, but I was wrong. And I was able to find the girl but not the briefcase myself."

I looked at him. "It's about time we got around to you," I said. "You know all about it without fitting in anywhere. Just how did you get into the act?"

"I didn't." I stared at him and he smiled back at me. "Let me put it this way, Mr. London. I learned of the situation. My livelihood hinges upon my ability to hear of situations where a profit is in the offing. I heard of this one, worked very carefully, found the girl out, and arrived too late on the scene. I'm still searching for the briefcase. I intend to make a spectacular profit when I get hold of it." His smile spread. "Does that answer your question?"

"I guess it has to."

He held out both hands. "My contribution," he said. "Now you must keep your part of the bargain. What do you know?"

"Not much."

"It may help. Will you tell me?"

I gave him most of it. I left out Jack Enright's name,

95

kept some of the details purposely vague. He listened to all of it.

"That helps," he said. "It explains things."

"It does?"

"Of course. I now understand several points which made no sense before. Your presence, for example. I had to think you were after the briefcase since there was no other explanation for your interest in Alicia. I also understand how she found an alias so easily. It was waiting for her because of her double life with your friend. Yes, it makes sense now."

There was silence for a few seconds. Maddy broke it. "You said you went to the apartment," she said to Armin. "Was that after Sheila . . . Alicia . . . was killed?"

"That's correct. After Mr. London's friend and before Mr. London. Say ten o'clock."

"And the apartment? What did it look like?"

He shrugged. "As Mr. London found it. The apartment neat, the girl garbed in stockings and garter belt. That's all."

"Just like that," I said.

"Just like that. I searched thoroughly, of course, but I left everything as I found it. A bizarre tableau. But I left it as it was."

"Then somebody was there after my friend and before you."

"Possibly."

"But——"

He said: "Not necessarily, though. Your friend, Mr. London, is neither criminal nor detective. He entered, reacted, left. He may have seen what you and I saw without it registering on his mind. You and I were emotionally stable, saw the scene as it was. But your friend must have been distraught——"

"He was a wreck."

"And consequently may have seen his mistress dead without seeing anything else. The death alone stayed in his memory. He arranged the rest unconsciously to conform with his vision of what should be, not what was."

96

"That's pretty far out, isn't it?"

"I'm not stating it as fact, Mr. London. Purely as a supposition. It makes a certain amount of sense, doesn't it?"

"Maybe."

"Think it through," he suggested. "The apartment was neat all along. Alicia was at home. Bannister or his men came in, searched the apartment, found nothing, killed her. Perhaps they molested her sexually. He employs that type of thug—"

I reminded him that there was no evidence.

"There doesn't have to be," he said. "She was hardly a virgin. Or suppose they stripped her to search her, if you prefer it that way. They killed her and left. Your friend came, saw, and ran screaming, his mind unhinged. I came, searched, and left. You came, removed the body, and went away with it."

His analysis was logical enough. I let it lie there. Something was a little out of whack but I could worry about it later.

I stood up, turned to Maddy. "Let's go," I said.

"Leaving?" He looked disappointed.

"Might as well," I said. "I'm going to see where I can get with Bannister. In the meantime you can work from the angle of the briefcase. With both of us handling opposite sides of the street we should double our chances of getting somewhere."

"We should."

"We've made progress already," I told him. "There's just one thing more."

I took out his Beretta, let him look at it. I think there was a second or two when he thought I was going to shoot him with it.

"This is yours," I said. "You might as well have it."

He did one hell of a take. He stared hard at me, then burst out laughing. He was a little guy but he laughed like a dynamo. It took him a few minutes before he could talk again.

"Oh, that's funny," he said. "That's really funny. But I still have the mate to that gun, Mr. London. And since we're working together I'd like you to keep that one for your own protection. You might need it."

He started laughing again. "But that's funny," he said. "That's really very funny."

TEN

WE left him laughing and rode the elevator down to the lobby. I stopped there to relight my pipe. I'm glad I did. Otherwise I probably would have missed him.

He was the kind of guy it's easy to miss. He sat in a big armchair and disappeared in it. He had his nose buried in a copy of the *Morning Telegraph* but his eyes showed over the top of it and they were looking at us.

We had a tail.

I finished lighting the pipe, took Maddy by the arm and steered her toward the door. I heard a rustle behind us as he started to fold up his paper. "Don't look around," I said, "but we've got a shadow. A little man who isn't there."

"How do we get rid of him?"

It's not hard to duck a shadow if you know he's there. You can tell your cabby to do some tricks with his hack, or you can walk in one entrance of a building and out another, or you can play games on the subway, getting off the car just before the doors close and letting your tail ride to Canarsie alone. But I didn't feel like just ducking the little bastard. He was Bannister's present to me and I wanted to send him home looking ugly. I was sick of Bannister and his presents.

"Could you stand a screen test?"

She didn't understand.

"You're an actress," I told her. "I've got a little acting for you to do. Game?"

I told her about it and she was game. We walked out of the Ruskin and down the block to Forty-third Street. We cornered at Forty-third and idled in a doorway, waiting for our friend to catch up with us. He was lousy.

He took the corner and breezed past us without spotting us.

Now we were tailing him.

He must have thought we were shuffling along ahead of him in the crowd. He kept on going, taking life easy, and we stayed with him all the way to Broadway.

Then Maddy went into her act.

We picked up a little speed and moved even with him, Maddy on the inside. Just as we moved into the mainstream of pedestrian traffic Maddy brushed up against him and let out a yell they could have heard in Secaucus. Everybody within three blocks turned and stared at her. The little guy stared, too, and his eyes popped halfway out of his pudgy head.

So it was my turn. I yelled: "You rotten son of a bitch!" Then I grabbed him with one hand and hit him with another. He bounced off the side of the building and looked at me with the sickest expression anybody ever had.

"Horrible," Maddy kept telling the world. "Dirty little pervert. Put his hands all over . . . oh, horrible!"

The jerk looked the part. He had runny eyes and a weak mouth and glasses half an inch thick. When I hit him the second time he lost the glasses. They landed on the sidewalk and somebody ground them into the pavement.

I was still hitting him when a cop turned up. He was big and rosily Irish and he wanted to know what the hell I was doing. I didn't have to tell him. The crowd—a big one, and all rooting for me, defender of chastity and feminine virtue—let him know just what was happening and why. He gave our shadow a very unhappy look.

"I could take him in," he said. "But it's a heap of trouble. You'd have to swear out a complaint and make an appearance in court. And I'd have to come in and testify. Work for everybody."

I commiserated with him.

"I'll tell you," the cop said. "Why don't you just belt him a few times and forget him? He won't pull a stunt like that again, I'll tell the world. And my eyes will be open for him from now on."

That sounded like a good idea. I stood the shadow up against the wall and hit him in the face. He lost a few teeth and his nose started to bleed.

"Tell Bannister to go to hell," I told him.

I hit him again. Then I piled Maddy into a cab and we left him there.

"I wish you'd put that thing away," Maddy was saying. "It scares me stiff."

I'd been checking the Beretta to make sure it was loaded. It was. I put it back together and gave it a pat, then dropped it back in my jacket pocket.

"Take off your jacket," she said. "Relax."

I hung my jacket on a doorknob and sank down again on the couch. We were in Maddy's apartment where the cab had dropped us. It was late.

"Poor Ed," she said. "How do you feel now?"

"Don't remind me."

"Bad?"

I nodded. "The cognac wore off," I said. "I can feel my stomach again. I should have stopped for a bottle."

"Look in the kitchen."

I gave her a long look, then stood up and went into the little kitchen. Red and white linoleum covered the floor. A gas stove sat in one corner and looked dangerous. An antique refrigerator sat in another corner and looked undependable. There was a rickety table between them, painted to match the linoleum, and on top of it there was a bottle of Courvoisier. A pint, unopened.

I picked it up gently and carried it back to the living room. Maddy had a smile on her face and a gleam in her eyes. "This," I said, "was not here yesterday."

"The great detective is right."

"And you're not much of a brandy drinker. You didn't buy this for your own consumption, Madeleine."

She blushed beautifully. "The detective is right again," she said. "I bought it this afternoon before I went detecting for you. I sort of hoped you'd be up here soon. Now pour yourself a drink while I sit here and feel wanton."

I opened the bottle and poured drinks for both of us.

101

I gave her about an ounce and filled my glass to the brim. I drank off some of the brandy and told my stomach it could relax now. Then I gave Maddy her glass and sat on the couch with her, sipping and smoking, while the world got better again.

She said: "You're not going home tonight."

I started to say something but she didn't give me a chance. "Don't flatter yourself, Ed. I don't have any designs on your virtue. Not in your condition. It would probably kill you."

"Sounds like——"

"——a good way to go. I know all about it. Don't hand me a hard time, Ed. You're staying here tonight. You can't go back to your apartment. You'd be a sitting duck and God knows how many people want to shoot you."

"Not too many," I told her. "I could always take a hotel room."

She said NO very emphatically. "It'll take you hours to find one and hours to fall asleep. And this is the best hotel in New York, Ed. Here you get congenial companionship, room and board, and the use of an untapped phone. What more could you ask for?"

"That's plenty. You make it sound sensible."

"It is sensible," she insisted. "And you're staying. Agreed?"

I agreed. I slipped an arm around her and took a sip of the cognac. I was getting tired but I didn't feel like sleep. I was too confortable to think about moving.

"I've got a feeling," she said suddenly. "I don't think you should be on that Peter Armin's side."

"Oh? I thought you liked him."

She bit her lip. "I do, kind of. But he's a crook, Ed. He wants to make an illegal profit on stolen jewels. If you get the briefcase back are you going to give it to him?"

"Uh-huh."

"Even though it's illegal?"

I took a sip of the cognac. "We made a bargain," I told her. "Besides, I'm looking for a killer. Not a batch of jewels. A murderer."

"But——"

"And the murderer's all I give a damn about," I went on. "Why in hell should I care what happens to the jewels? Armin's as much entitled to them as anybody else. Who do they belong to? Wallstein's dead and buried. His widow shouldn't get them—they weren't his to give her and she wasn't married to him legally, anyway. The original owners are either dead or lost. Who's next in line? The government of Argentina, as a reward for harboring a Nazi?"

I took a breath. "I don't care about them. Armin may be as crooked as a corkscrew. As far as I'm concerned he's welcome to the briefcase and the jewels and whatever he can get out of this mess. All I care about is a killer."

"Then why did you ask for five thousand dollars?"

"Because otherwise he would have thought I was insane. And because Bannister's boys ruined my home and my appetite. I've been shot at and followed and slugged. Hell, I don't have a client—I might as well get a little compensation one way or the other. I can use five grand."

She nodded, digesting this. I couldn't tell whether she approved or not. Hell, I'm not a plaster saint. Single men in barracks don't grow into them.

"What I wonder now," I said, "is how much of Armin's story is true."

"You think he lied?"

"I'm sure he lied. It's a question of degree." I shrugged. "I can't swallow that routine of his about being a clever operator waiting in the wings to make a neat profit. It's too damned cute. I'd like to know where he fits in."

"Any ideas, Mr. London, sir?"

"A couple," I said. "Notice how formal he is? You're not the only one who calls me 'Mr. London.' He's never called me anything else. He even refers to our boy Clay as 'Mr. Bannister'."

"It's a common affectation, Ed."

"Sure. But Sheila-Alicia was always just plain 'Alicia' to him. I've got a hunch he knew her when. Think back a minute. He talked about her almost reminiscently. Remember?"

"I didn't notice. But now that you mention it. . . ."

I grinned. "Now that I mention it, I think he's one of the jewel thieves. Or Alicia's buddy from the past, hooking up with her again to pull a quick one."

We sat there thinking that one over. I got my pipe going again, worked on the cognac. "One thing comes first," I told her. "The briefcase. Nobody's got it and it's in the middle of everything. I think I'll ring up Jack Enright tomorrow."

"Why?"

"Because I think I can pry a little more out of him. The girl must have been nervous as all hell just after she pulled the rug out from under Bannister. She may have dropped a hint or two about the briefcase."

"But he said——"

"I know what he said. Memory's a tricky proposition. I'm going to try him on Armin's theory about the apartment, then on the briefcase. He may be able to remember a little more now. His big concern now is keeping himself in the clear and preserving the harmony of his happy home. His memory might work better now that he's had a day or two to cool off."

She took my pipe from my mouth and placed it in an ashtray. "Speaking of which," she cooed, "it's time for you to cool yourself off. You've been through the wringer today, Ed. Drink up your brandy and we'll go to bed."

I leered lecherously.

"To sleep," she said. "Not to bed. To sleep."

I finished the brandy.

Her bed was soft and welcome, the sheets cool and clean. I let my head sink into the pillow and opened my eyes to look at darkness. Water was running in the bathroom. I pictured her washing her face, brushing her teeth, drying herself with a towel.

Pretty pictures.

The bedroom door opened inward. The light was behind her and I saw her slender body silhouetted in the door frame. She touched a switch and the light died. She came into the room, closed the door behind her. I could barely see her in the darkness.

104

"Ed?"

I didn't answer her.

I heard a nightgown rustle. She lifted the covers on her side of the bed and slid under them. "Goodnight, Ed," she whispered. "Sleep well. I'll make breakfast for you in the morning, Ed."

I still didn't say anything. I heard her breathing beside me, sensed the sweet warmth of her body. I remembered that body, remembered the night before.

I reached for her.

For an instant she gasped, surprised. Then my mouth found hers and we kissed. I took her shoulders in my hands and felt her body begin to tremble.

"Oh," she said. "Oh, Ed. Ed, we can't, not tonight, Ed. You're all tired and all hurt and we can't. Ed—"

I ran a hand over her body, all clean and soft and warm through the sheer nightgown.

"We can't, Ed. Ed, darling, we can't, I want to, I want to but we can't."

I put my face to her cheek and breathed the fragrance of her hair. I kissed her again and heard her sigh.

"We can't," she said. "We can't we can't we can't we can't—"

I drew her body very close to mine. I whispered softly into her ear.

"We can," I said. "And we will."

We did.

She amazed me in the morning. She scrambled eggs and fried bacon and toasted rye bread, and she didn't even try to talk to me until I was working on my second cup of strong black coffee. I had never known a woman could behave so magnificently in the morning, or look so lovely. I told her this and she beamed at me.

"The phone," she said. "You were going to call Enright."

I picked up the receiver and dialed his number. A female voice found out who I was and told me to hold the line. I did. Then Jack picked up the phone.

"Ed, Jack. I've got to talk to you. Important."

He said: "Oh, Christ." Then he didn't say anything

for a minute or two. A juvenile voice wailed unhappily in the background. "I'm busy as all hell right now, Ed. You at home? I'll call you as soon as I get a free moment."

I told him where I was and he took down the number. "Stay there," he said. "I may be a while. Bye, Ed."

I told Maddy he'd be calling back. We cleared off the table. She washed the dishes and I dried them. Then we sat around waiting for the phone to ring, with the whole scene so damned domestic that I couldn't stand it. Finally the phone came through for me and I stood up to answer it.

"It might be for me," she said. "I'll take it."

I was already at the phone.

"Please," she said. "You'll compromise me."

"You've already been compromised. And after the way you kept saying we couldn't. You were wrong."

"So you're Superman. Now . . . hey, let go of me, you oaf! It's the middle of the murky morning and the phone's ringing. Let go!"

I got out of the way. She answered the phone while I stood by, waiting for her to hand it to me when Jack identified himself. This didn't happen.

The phone was for her and I listened while she talked to somebody named Maury. She spent most of her time listening, tossing in an occasional uh-huh. Then she made scribbling motions in the air until I brought her a scrap of paper and a pencil. She took them and began jotting down mysterious information. This went on for a few minutes, until finally she said: Thanks, sweetie at least four times and kissed the telephone mouthpiece twice. Then she hung up and turned to me, her eyes bright.

"It was Maury," she said.

"Thanks. Who's Maury?"

"My agent. And Lon Kaspar's auditioning for the lead in 'The House of Bernardo Alba,' it's the Lorca play and they're doing a revival over on Second Avenue and it's this afternoon and Maury thinks I've got a great chance and—"

She ran out of breath before she ran out of words. I asked her when she had to be at the theater.

106

"Eleven-thirty, if I can. What time is it?"

"Quarter to eleven."

"What!"

"We slept late and ate slowly and graciously. You better hurry, Maddy. But don't you get to study the part?"

"It's just a reading today. Oh, God, I've got to rush. God, I have to hurry. It's all the way across town, dammit. You wait here for your phone call, Ed. The door locks by itself when you close it. I have to rush."

I kissed her. She held onto me for a minute, then pulled away. "Dammit to hell," she said. "I wanted to stay with you today. I thought we could hunt the killer together. Then this came up."

"I wouldn't have let you come along."

"You couldn't have stopped me. But one little call from Maury . . . damn."

I grinned. "Is it a good part?"

"It's a beautiful part," she said. "Simply beautiful. And Maury thinks I can get it. He says Kaspar knows me and likes my work. I've got to run, Ed. One call on the old phone and away goes Maddy. I'll be home sometime this afternoon, I think. Call me."

She was still talking on her way out the door, still bubbling and babbling as she went down the stairs. From the front window I watched her hail a cab. My smile followed her down the street.

A sweet kid.

I poured a third cup of coffee and sweetened it with a taste of cognac. I lit a cigarette to go with it.

A hell of a sweet kid.

I thought about Jack Enright. I thought about Kaye, his wife and my sister. Evenings at their place, the three of us plus whatever girl Kaye was tying to fix me up with at the time. "You ought to get married, Ed London. It's no life for a man, being a bachelor. You should meet a nice girl and settle down."

And I thought about Maddy, and how sweet she was in the morning, and how sweet she was at night. And Kaye's words made more sense than they ever had before.

Which scared me.

The phone rang half an hour after Maddy left. I answered it. It was Jack.

"Sorry I had to hang up on you," he said. "I was up to my neck in work and I didn't want to talk on that phone of mine. I'm on a pay phone now. Is your line safe?"

I told him it was.

"Did you see the paper, Ed? They had a bit about Sheila. That she was involved with some gangsters and they killed her."

I wondered where they got that. "They're right," I said.

"Then why not let it go? You know how those men operate. Fly a killer in from the other side of the country, then fly him away when he's done. You can't solve a crime like that. Why knock yourself out trying? Why waste time?"

"You all worried about my time, Jack?"

A sigh. "All right," he said. "Okay, I'm scared. If you come up with anything you'll have to give it all to the police. Then everything's out in the open. I'm scared, Ed. I've got a lot of things to be scared about. A family and a practice. I don't want them to blow up in my face."

"I can keep you out of it."

"Can you?"

"Uh-huh. And I couldn't let go even if I wanted to, Jack. Two heavies handed me a beating yesterday. Another guy was tailing me. Somebody else missed me with a bullet a while back. I've been on one end or the other of enough handguns to win the West ten times over. So I can't leave it alone."

"God," he said. "They're trying to scare you?"

"They're trying to get a briefcase from me. I don't have it."

"Who does?"

"I don't know. Jack, didn't Sheila ever mention anything about a briefcase? Anything about jewels or criminals?"

"No. Never. Let me think." I let him think. "Never," he said flatly. "I told you what she talked about. There was never anything about a briefcase or jewels or crooks."

108

I let go of it. "About the apartment," I said, shifting. "When you found Sheila. Maybe you were mistaken, maybe the apartment was neat and Sheila was naked and your mind did a little dance with itself. You were under a strain, Jack. You might not have seen things the way they were. Hell, you're a doctor. You know how the human mind can react to shock."

I listened to heavy breathing. Then: "You think you and I saw the apartment the same way."

"That's right."

He hesitated. "That's been bothering me," he said finally. "I almost called you last night. I wanted to tell you about it."

"Want to tell me now?"

"It's just a feeling I had."

"Go on."

He said: "I was thinking about the murder. The way I found the body. I went over it in my mind and it didn't seem to mesh together properly. Do you know what I mean? I had a certain distant memory—a dead girl, Sheila, and a messed-up apartment, and all that. But somewhere in the back of my mind was the idea that it wasn't that way at all. There was a conflicting picture that hadn't been there before. A picture of Sheila nude and dead in the middle of a neat apartment. I don't know if the second picture is real or if it stuck in my mind when you described it to me. It could be either way."

"I see."

"I'm not sold on it one way or the other," he went on. "But if you've got a hunch I was seeing things, well, I'll go along with you. It makes sense to me."

I said something innocuous. He told me again that he hoped I'd keep him out of it and I said I'd do my best. We spent a few seconds looking around for something to say to each other, then settled on "So long" and ended the conversation. I held onto the receiver and studied it, trying to think clearly. Then I put it down and poured the last of Maddy's coffee into my cup.

The conversation with Jack hadn't proved anything one way or the other. He was too busy trying to forget forever the fact that he had managed to commit adultery and get mixed up in a murder. Now all he cared about was staying in the clear and smelling like a rose. Anything he said or did was going to be colored by that desire. He'd go along with any theory I came up with just to keep things simple.

I finished the coffee, washed out my cup and put it away. I found a broom and gave the apartment a quick sweeping. I wrote Maddy a note, then read it over and decided it was painfully cute. I tore it up and wrote her a blander one, put it on the rickety kitchen table and set the brandy bottle on top of it.

At the door I turned to take a last look at the apartment and think pleasant thoughts about the girl who lived in it. Then I went down two flights, passing Madame Sindra and the machine shop, and out onto the street.

The sun was high in the sky and the air was hot. I managed to snag a cab on Eight Avenue. I sat back and gave my home address to the driver, letting him fight the traffic.

A few points bothered me. Both Armin and Bannister knew I went to the girl's apartment. They sure as hell didn't pool information between them. Which meant both of them had seen me.

How?

They couldn't both have kept the apartment under surveillance at the same time. They both knew I went there, but neither one knew I didn't come out with the briefcase.

Why?

I tossed it around and didn't get anywhere with it. I lit my pipe while the cab clawed its way through the beginnings of the noon rush hour. My cabby inched his way north on Eighth Avenue, jockeying for position with Puerto Rican boys pushing hand trucks of ladies' dresses. I sat and smoked.

The city was getting hotter as the day rolled along. Maddy was reading for a good part; I was chasing a briefcase and a killer. A good day.

When we hit Forty-second Street I started wondering about my own apartment. I lost the thought when we passed the Ruskin and Peter Armin came back to mind. I got back to it a few blocks along the line and wondered what sort of a job Cora Johnson had been able to do. And how much of the damage was permanent.

And how well five grand would compensate for it.

My stomach-ache wasn't bothering me. Ralph and Billy still were, though. I sat there and remembered. And hated them.

I reached into my pocket. The Beretta was still there, small and sleek and deadly. I stroked cool metal and thought about Ralph and Billy.

I climbed stairs to my apartment, lifted a corner of my Welcome mat—which says Go Away, incidentally—and picked up my key. This was one of Cora's less logical habits; she couldn't believe I had two keys to my own apartment and always left the damned key precisely where I had left it for her. This always gave me a bad moment. I couldn't be sure whether she'd been there or not until I opened the door.

I bent over again, scooped up the *Times*. I straightened up, stuck key in lock, held my breath, and pushed. She had been there.

I thanked her silently. The place looked livable again. Hell, it looked great—each book was back in the book-case, the rugs were clean, the furniture polished. I closed the door and tossed my newspaper on a chair. There would be time to read it later on. Now it was more fun to look around.

Some of the books were still ruined, of course. A book-maker could patch up most of them as soon as I had time to run them in. And the chair cushions were still slit open. But Cora had done one beautiful hell of a job. I took a deep breath, feeling very pleased with the world in general and with Cora Johnson in particular.

Only one thing was out of whack. I looked at it and the room started to spin around. I stood there with my mouth wide open and my stupid face hanging out.

There was a tan cowhide briefcase on the coffee table and it had never been there before.

111

ELEVEN

I WENT to the shelf and poured a little cognac in one of the glasses. I drank it off and turned around.

The briefcase was still there.

One of the slick mags had a feature running a few years back under the title "What's Wrong With This Picture?" The pitch was quietly mindless—a Mona Lisa frowning on a wall, a man with two left hands, a face without eyebrows. The reader was upposed to puzzle it out, figure out what was wrong.

Hell, it was easy. The briefcase was wrong. It wasn't supposed to be there at all, and there it was.

It should have been funny as hell. By the time I finally managed to sell Armin on the idea that I never had the case to begin with, wham—there it was. For a crazy second or two I wondered if it had been there all along, if Cora had unearthed it for me while she straightened up. That little piece of insanity didn't last long. Somebody had brought the briefcase there while I was out. Somebody had given me a present.

Why?

I wasn't going to worry about whys just then. I went to the door, locked it and slid the bolt home. I took the briefcase from the coffee table and sat down in a chair to examine it. I turned it over and over in my hands like a little kid with a Christmas present trying to guess what was inside. I shook it to see if it would rattle. It didn't.

I: was well-made and it was expensive. The leather was top-grain quality, the stitching neat and precise. It looked like an English job, which fit Armin's little story about Canadian jewel thieves. But since most of the better briefcases sold in the States are English ones, it really didn't mean too much one way or the other. So there was nothing to do but open the thing. So I opened it.

The inside had more things going for it. There was a long and detailed letter typed flawlessly on plain white bond. It bore no date, no return address, no signature. It led off with a simple "Dear Sir" and went on from there.

The instructions were complicated. Two keys were supposed to be in the briefcase. One, according to the letter, would fit a small locker in Central Terminal in Buffalo, New York. There was a strongbox in that locker, and the second key would open the strongbox. The box itself contained still another key, this one fitting a locker located in a station of the Toronto subway system. That locker, finally, held the Wallstein jewels.

The nameless person who wrote the letter apologized very carefully for the complexity of the directions. He was sure, he said, that the reader would appreciate them. By use of two lockers plus a strongbox, a man with keys but without instructions would be lost. So would any outsider who happened to break into the Buffalo locker—he'd find a meaningless key. If somebody was lucky enough to break into the Toronto locker he'd get the jewels, but nobody would know which Toronto locker to open unless he had the instructions in the first place and the key in the second—the key from the Buffalo locker.

I had to read the damned thing three times through before I could figure out which key was which and what the hell it was all about. By the time it made sense I had to admire whoever figured it all out. Nothing was left to chance. And there was another advantage—in the time it took to follow all the directions, the thieves would be out of town. And safe.

It was cute. But for all the good it had done the thieves they could have filled the briefcase with jewels and let it go at that. Bannister had managed to put them all in the river—except for Armin, possibly—and to get his dough back at the same time. Proving, maybe, that the best laid plans of jewel thieves gang aft aglay. They're in the same boat with the mice and the men. And it leaked like a sieve.

113

So now I had the briefcase. The next step, according to the book, was to turn it over to Peter Armin and collect a quick five thousand dollars for my troubles. Somehow I couldn't quite see myself doing this. Not just yet. I had told Maddy the truth—my main interest was catching a killer and I didn't care who Armin was or what he did with the jewels. But the briefcase might be useful to me. Maybe I could catch a murderer with it. Armin could wait a day or two for his briefcase and I could wait a day or two for my money. The killer came first.

I looked at the briefcase with respect. It was a bomb that could go off any minute, a nitro bomb that would behave unpredictably. I decided to dismantle it.

I staggered through the directions again. It was the fourth time around for me and this time I memorized them. There wasn't all that much to remember. Just a pair of locker numbers. When they were tucked away in my mind I found a sheet of typing paper and hauled out my old portable. I copied the letter word for word, substituting new and meaningless numbers for the original ones. Then I tore the original letter into little strips of paper and flushed them down the toilet. I felt like a character in a bad Mitchum movie.

I found the pair of keys in a pocket in the briefcase. There numbers had been filed off and they looked innocent as vestal virgins. I replaced them with two keys of my own. One of them would open the door to a place in Greenwich Village where I'd lived years ago. Another would open the door to an apartment where a girl I once knew once lived. She was married now, and she didn't live there any more. So I didn't need the key.

I filed the sides of both keys, put them in the pocket of the briefcase, zipped it shut. I added the new set of phony instructions and closed the briefcase.

My bomb was a dud now.

I remembered telling Maddy something about bombs, saying they were going to start going off, that I wanted to set off a few of my own. I wondered if you could set off a dead bomb, a dud.

It was worth a try.

The kid with all the pimples was scratching himself. He looked up at me and gave me something that was almost a smile. Then he found my car and turned it over to me.

"I thought you just worked nights."

"Usually," he said. "Like today I'm working days. Win a few; lose a few. Today's a good day for a convertible. You can roll down the top and look at the sunshine."

"Uh-huh. Want to fill the tank?"

He studied the gauge. "Not worth the sweat," he said. "She's almost full now, see? You got to do a lot of driving to empty her, a whole lot. I can fill her when you bring her in."

"I'll be doing a lot of driving."

"Well——"

"Fill the tank," I said.

He filled the tank but he didn't have his heart in it. I told him to put it on the tab, pulled out of the garage and left him scratching and mumbling. I felt better with a full tank of gas. It's one of two prerequisites for a trip to the end of Long Island. The second is courage.

I took Second Avenue south, found the Queens Midtown Tunnel and left the relative sanity of Manhattan for the hinterlands of Queens. I followed a variety of confusing expressways—which is where the courage came into the picture—until I managed to pass through Queens, rush through Nassau County and wind up in Suffolk County.

If you've got enough money, and if you don't like New York, and if Westchester and Connecticut are either too arty or too Madison Avenue for you, you stand a good chance of winding up in Suffolk County. The towns were smaller there, the buildings lower and further apart. I had the top down and the fresh air was choking me. My lungs weren't used to it.

I drove through the countryside and tried to pretend that it wasn't really there. I remembered a line out of Sydney Smith to the effect that the country is sort of a healthy grave. Sydney Smith was right.

Bannister, according to Armin, lived in something called Avalon. I had copied down his address on the back of the

115

snapshot Armin gave me, and when I hit Avalon I pulled over to the curb and fumbled through my wallet until I found it. I looked at it, remembered what Bannister was supposed to look like, then turned the photo over and checked the address. He lived on Emory Hill Road.

There was gas still left in the tank but there was room for more. A gas-pump jockey loaded me up without an argument, polished my windshield, checked my oil and water, and tried to sell me a new fuel pump. He also told me how to get to Emory Hill Road. It ran along the outskirts of Avalon. Living on the outskirts of Avalon is like living in a suburb of New Jersey, or a satellite of the moon. It's ridiculous.

I followed his directions, found Emory Hill Road. I nosed the Chevy past a batch of estates that would have embarrassed Veblen. They were all the last word on the subject of conspicuous consumption. I passed them all by until I found one which made the rest look like Tobacco Road set to music. It had to belong to Clayton Bannister. Nobody else would want it.

First there was the house itself. The manor house, that is—I'm sure that's what he called it. It was a cock-eyed cross between Christopher Wren and Le Corbusier, a mixed marriage of the seventeenth and twentieth centuries with the assets of neither and the liabilities of both. I had never seen anything like it before; twentieth-century baroque was a brand-new concept. Flying buttresses do not go with picture windows.

The architect must have shot himself.

There were two other small houses. One must have been the guest house. The other was the garage but it looked more like a stable. A futuristic stable, of course, but still a stable. I saw a Rolls Silver Ghost and a Mercedes 300 and tried to imagine Bannister at the wheel riding to hounds, with Ralph and Billy bellowing "Tallyho!" at the tops of their impure lungs. An arresting picture.

I parked the Chevy in front of the estate and looked around for a chrome-and-steel hitching post. There should have been one, but there wasn't. I yanked the emergency brake, killed the ignition and got out of the car. I

116

looked at carefully landscaped grounds covered with too many different kinds of shrubs and flowers. He'd have done better cultivating one small garden.

I filled a pipe and got it going. I dropped the match onto the lawn and hoped it would start a fire. Then, briefcase tucked under arm, I started up the road to hell. It was paved with flagstones instead of good intentions.

When I was about thirty yards from the manor house its carved oak door burst open and a gorilla exploded out of it, gun in hand. It was Billy. He ran quickly and awkwardly and stopped a yard away from me.

"Whatcha want?"

I said: "Take me to your leader."

"Huh?"

"The boss," I said patiently. "I want to see the boss."

When he looked as though he understood, I held up the briefcase. "For the boss," I said. "A present." He reached out a paw to snatch it away but I pulled it back and smiled sadly. "Not for you, Billy Boy. For the boss. Mr. Bannister. The king."

He was still mulling that one over when the other half of the goon squad appeared. Ralph. He walked up quickly, his face a mask, took the gun away from Billy and listened to my speech.

"Go tell the boss who's here and what he wants," he told Billy. "I'll stay here and watch him."

He stayed there and watched me while Billy hurried home with the message to Garcia. We had nothing to say to each other so we stood and glared away. He kept the gun on me and looked as though he wanted me to move so he could put a hole in my stomach. I didn't and it made him unhappy.

He broke the silence.

"What I figure," he said, "is the boss'll tell Billy to tell me to take the briefcase away from you and send you home."

I didn't answer him.

"What I figure," he went on, "is you want him to pay you for it. It's stupid, you ask me. He woulda paid you before, when he asked you. You weren't selling. You were so smart and you had to get beat up, now you come

117

to sell to him? He can kick you out on your ear. You could of saved yourself a drive, you could of put it in the mail or called up and said come and get it. You don't make sense."

I didn't answer him. A bird sang songs in a nearby tree. The wind rustled leaves in other trees. The big carved oak door opened and Billy's big head appeared.

He called: "The boss says bring him in."

Ralph managed to register surprise without changing expression. A neat trick. He nodded slowly, then stepped aside and motioned with the gun. I looked at the gun. It was bigger than the Beretta in my pocket.

"You go inside," he said. "I walk behind you; I keep this pointed at you. Don't get fancy."

I didn't get fancy. There were three marble steps at the head of the flagstone path. I climbed them and walked through the open door into the room. Billy pointed through another doorway and led me through to the living room. I followed with Ralph right behind and felt like meat in a sandwich.

The living room had thick wall-to-wall carpeting and a beamed ceiling. The beams were huge. They almost gave the room the air of a cathedral, but misfired slightly. The furniture was large and heavy and ugly. There were books in a bookcase, all expensively bound, mostly in sets, all, undoubtedly, unread.

I looked at the room. I looked at Ralph and Billy, both standing in front of me now. I looked at Ralph's gun.

And I looked at Clayton Bannister.

He didn't look like his picture now. His baldness didn't show because he was the world's first country squire to wear his hat in his house. He also wore light gray flannel slacks, a red plaid hunting shirt open at the throat and expensive shoes. He had a large cigar in his mouth and he talked around it.

"You're tough to figure," he said. "You're supposed to be tough and you're supposed to be smart and I don't think you're either one. What's the bit, London?"

"I brought you a present."

"And you think you'll get paid for it? You had your chance, dumbhead. You know what I woulda paid for that briefcase. Twenty grand. Maybe thirty. Now I get it for nothing, dumbhead."

I fingered the briefcase. "You'd pay me twenty grand," I said. "Then you'd send some boys around to take the money back and blow my brains out. That's smart?"

His face darkened. "A cutie," he said. "Don't get cute. I don't like it. You gonna give me that thing?"

I tossed it to him. He caught it with surprising grace for a man of his bulk. He opened it with his eyes on me, then lowered his gaze to study the contents. He read the letter quickly, nodding from time to time to prove he could read. Then he looked up.

"Where's the keys?"

"In the pouch with the zipper."

"They better be," he said darkly. He opened the zippered compartment and took out the keys. He studied them, smiled with obvious pleasure, put them back in the pouch, zipped it shut, put the letter back, zipped the briefcase and tossed the whole thing onto an overstuffed sofa.

"You know what it's all about, London?"

"Jewels," I said.

"Smart boy. Just jewels?"

"The Wallstein jewels."

"Very smart boy." He took the cigar from his mouth and pointed at me with it, looking at Ralph and Billy as he did so. They stood on either side of him, Ralph with his gun drawn, Billy with his apey arms at his sides.

"This is a smart boy," he told them. "You look at this boy; you listen to him; he's smart. You hear how he talks? He talks better than you two put together. He talks better than me and I'm not so damn stupid. He's what you call cultured."

He sighed. "But he's still a dumbhead. You see?"

They both nodded dutifully.

"You," he said. "London. You take a good look at this place? The house and the grounds? You check out the trees and furniture and all?"

"I saw them."

"Whattaya think?"

"Impressive," I said.

"Impressive," he echoed. He thought it was a compliment. "You think I know a goddam thing about architecture? I know what I like, anybody knows that, but that's all. You see that picture on the wall? It's by Matisse. What I know about art you can put in your ear. What I know about Matisse you can put in the same ear and have room left. I bet you know a hell of a lot about architecture. And about art. I bet you know about Matisse. Right?"

"Some."

"I also bet you don't have a house like this one," he said. "I also bet you don't have a Matisse hanging on the wall. I don't mean a goddam copy. I mean what they call an original. Right?"

I told him he was right. I didn't bother telling him I wouldn't live in his house on a bet or that I didn't like Matisse. This would have annoyed him.

"I got and you don't, London. You know why?"

"Money, probably."

"Part right. Money and power. I want a house, I go hire an architect and tell him what I want. I want a good picture, I call a dealer and tell him I want the best. That's why I got this briefcase."

He walked over to a heavy mahogany drum table with ugly claw feet. He ground his cigar to a pulp in an ashtray. He came back and pointed at me, this time with his finger.

"You got to get the point of this, London. You had the briefcase and I wanted it. I offered to pay you off. You, you had to be smart. Too smart. You didn't want to play. Money wasn't enough, so power came in. I sent a little muscle to show you I wasn't playing games. The muscle knocked the crap out of you. The muscle told you you could get your head knocked-in playing cute. So now I got the briefcase and you got nothing."

I looked at him.

"Muscle," he said reverently. "How long you think you'd have a President without an army? Or a business. You take when they started labor unions. The workers, the slobs, went out on strike. They wouldn't work. So the boss, he got some muscle going for him. He hired some slobs and told them to break a few heads. All of a sudden there wasn't a strike any more. Everybody was working."

I told him the unions were still around. He looked at me scornfully. "You know why? They got smart. They got muscle of their own and they broke heads on their own. You see?"

I nodded. I looked at Billy, the muscle we were batting back and forth. He looked muscle-bound and stupid. I looked at Ralph. He was more of a right arm than a muscle. He looked useful and his gun looked dangerous. More dangerous than my Beretta. I wondered if it was the same gun he killed the blonde with.

"And you're the smart one," he was saying. "So I got the briefcase and you got crap. I don't have to pay you a penny, London. You know what I can do now? I can tell Ralph to shoot a hole in your head. Not in here —why mess up the place, get the rug bloody?"

"You got the girl's rug bloody."

He gave me an odd look. "We take you outside," he went on. "Billy tells you to go outside and you go because he tells you and you don't want another beating. Then Ralph shoots a hole in you and Billy digs a deep hole and buries you. The gardner plants flowers."

He laughed, his heavy body shaking. "Better," he said. "We take you outside and we hand you a shovel and tell you to dig. We tell you you're digging your own grave and you dig it, anyhow. You think you wouldn't dig it? You think you can't make a man do any damn thing in the world?"

He was probably right.

"We tell you to dig and you dig. We tell you to lie down and you lie down. And then we shoot you and cover you up and plant the flowers and you disappear. Nobody ever knows what happened to you; you're gone. You never were in the first place."

I nodded slowly. "All because of power."

"You got it, London."

"Muscle," I said. "There's only one thing wrong with having muscle working for you."

"What's that?"

121

"The kind of person you have to have around."

"You mean Billy?"

"I mean Billy." I took a deep breath and wondered if they would really make me dig my own grave, and if I was really weak enough to do it.

"I mean Billy," I repeated, looking at the gorilla. "You know about him?"

He looked puzzled.

I looked at Billy and remembered the kind of punch he threw. I thought about what Ralph had said before, remembered how Billy had reacted. And wondered if it still worked that way.

"About him and his mother," I said, loud. "He sleeps with his mother, Bannister. He does things with her. Bad things."

And that was Billy's cue.

He came in high and he came in hard and he came in fast. I saw him coming, saw Ralph raise his gun behind him and take aim. Ralph wasn't going to shoot. He didn't figure it would be necessary. He was waiting.

So was I.

It happened quickly. Billy was hunting for my head and he threw a big fist at it. I ducked and let the punch go over my shoulder, then came up underneath him and pivoted. That lifted him up and spun him around. His own tremendous forward motion did all the rest of it.

And I threw him at Ralph.

He had come in high and hard and fast and he went out the same way, flying straight for Ralph. The little man —the right arm—went overbackwards with the big man on top of him. Maybe Ralph was trying to shoot me. Maybe the gun went off by accident, a pure reflex action.

It didn't matter. Either way it went off, a loud noise only slightly muffled by Billy's bulk. Either way Billy's T shirt turned red with his blood. Then the two of them hit the floor with an impact as loud as the gun shot. They did not move.

I looked from them to Bannister. He had a gun in his hand. It was a big gun and it was pointed at me.

TWELVE

IT was so quiet I could hear the country noises outside. Birds singing, crickets chirping, the wind in the trees. A scene of pastoral bliss. I looked at him, then at the gun and then at him again.

"That's the trouble with muscle," I said. "It can work both ways. Billy's muscle just got him killed."

The gun didn't waver. The mouth smiled but the eyes were colder than Death.

"Cute," he said. "Very cute. What was that? Judo?"

"Something like that."

"Using his own muscle against him," he said slowly. "Yeah, I get it. I had a Jap working for me once, little guy skinny as a bird. He could get cute like that, toss a guy my size clear across the room and off the wall. You know what you just did?"

I let him tell me.

"Same thing as Billy," he said. "You used your brains against you. You got so cute that in a minute or so I shoot you and you're dead. Your brains get blown out. What good are they then?"

I put my hands in my jacket pockets and tried to look casual about it. The Beretta was right where it was supposed to be. I tried not to think what would have happened if Ralph or Billy had taken it away from me. It was better not to think about things like that.

"You'd kill me anyway," I told him. "What's the difference?"

"Maybe. Maybe not."

"Sure you would. You've got enough killings under your belt. One more wouldn't hurt you."

He laughed like a clown. "Dumbhead," he said. "I

haven't killed anybody all by myself in fourteen years. You'll be the first. Unless Ralphie wakes up to save me the trouble."

I looked at Ralph and decided he wouldn't wake up for a while. "So you don't pull the trigger yourself," I said. "You order the hits instead. It's the same thing."

He didn't answer.

"You're just a killer, Bannister. You killed a batch of jewel thieves to save yourself a hundred grand. You killed a girl when she crossed you. Now I'm next. Congratulations."

He looked amused. I kept my hands in my pockets. My right hand closed around the Beretta and my index finger looked around for the trigger and found it. I was glad now that it was such a small gun. It made a neat bulge in the pocket, small enough so that he didn't even notice it.

"You're a pig," I said. "With all your money and all your power you're still fresh from the gutter. And the gutter smell clings to you. It won't wash off. You'll go on killing like an animal and living like an animal until somebody blows your brains out. Or until they strap you in the chair and throw the switch."

He wasn't Billy and he didn't get angry. His voice came out low and flat. It rasped like chalk on a blackboard.

He said: "Dumbhead. You know what you got for brains? You got crap for brains. Every time you try to get smart you get dumber and dumber."

"Really?"

"Yeah, really, you stupid bastard. You think I order a hit for the hell of it? Anybody kills for nothing is stupid. Those snatch-and-grab boys got hit because they crossed me. Somebody crosses you, you have to hit him. They came to me and asked a hundred grand for a batch of jewels. I paid their price and they tried to cut and run. No jewels for me. So they got hit and the dough came back where it belonged."

"What about the girl?"

He looked at me. "Alicia?"

I nodded.

124

He laughed and his big shoulders shook. "Dumber and dumber," he said. "We never hit the girl. Why hit her?"

"Because she double-crossed you."

"That broad crossed everybody," he said. "She was in line for a hit. But why cool her before I got the briefcase from her? The hell, I didn't even know where she was hiding out. She disappeared fast."

"Then how did you know I had the briefcase? If you didn't know where she lived, you didn't see me coming out of her apartment. So how did you spot me?"

"I didn't."

"You had a tail on me last night," I said. "I sent him home with his head in a sling. How did he pick me up?"

"You're in the wrong world, London. I didn't have you tailed."

I remembered a little mousy man with glasses. "A little guy. He picked me up at the Ruskin, where Armin is staying. And then——"

His smile spread around some more. "Is that where he's staying?"

"You already knew that, Bannister."

"I guess I know it now. Thanks."

I shifted gears again. It was cuter than hell—the more I knew, the more things got jumbled up all over again. "You didn't spot me with Alicia's body," I said. "But you figured I had the briefcase. Right?"

"Right."

"Then——"

My ignorance had him so happy I thought he was going to start giggling any minute. "So goddamn dumb," he said. "I got a phone call. You learn a lot of things over a phone. I learned you had the briefcase. And you did. So?"

"Who called you?"

"A little bird. You ask a lot of questions, you know that? What do you care about answers? I shoot you and you're dead. You believe there's a thing like heaven?"

"No."

He nodded swiftly. "Good. Neither do I. So you're dead, and when you're dead it's all over. In an hour or so you get stiff. Your hands and feet turn white. Powder

125

white, fishbelly white. A couple days after that you start to rot. And whatever you got going for you in your head, whatever your brains are loaded with, it rots too. The questions and the answers—they rot. Why ask?"

"Curiosity."

"It killed a lot of cats, London."

I took very careful aim with the Beretta. He was right but his reasons were all wrong. I didn't need any more questions and answers. I had all the answers that mattered. There were a few questions left here and there but Bannister wasn't going to be able to answer them.

Everything was coming into focus now. Everything was taking shape and working itself out.

I didn't need Clay Bannister any more.

"Dead," he was saying now. "Didn't have to kill you before. No point. Hell, you did me a favor. I take the briefcase and toss you out. What can you do to me? Nothing. You don't have a story to take to the cops and you're too small to give me a hard time on your own. I brush you away like a horse brushes flies."

"You can still do that."

He shook his big head. "Uh-uh," he grunted. "You killed one of my boys."

"Ralph killed him."

"Uh-uh. You killed him. So now it's your turn for some of the same. You still sure you don't believe in heaven? You want to squeeze in a round of last-minute praying?"

He could have gone on that way for another half hour. His voice was ugly but he liked the sound of it, liked the way his neo-Nietzschean crap rolled off his tongue. He might still be talking no . But I was sick of listening to him, sick of staring into the muzzle of his gun.

I steadied the Beretta and squeezed the trigger.

For a little gun it made one hell of a noise. Bannister's face started to change expression from satisfaction to horror. He got halfway there and wound up wearing a silly half-smile. I wondered how long it would take the undertaker to wipe it off his face.

I was aiming for his face but the bullet came in low. It took him in the neck, right in the center of the throat,

126

and he fell in slow motion, the gun in his hand all the way to the floor. When he was on his knees he squeezed the trigger in a death grip and a bullet plowed a furrow in the thick carpet.

He fell the rest of the way, then stopped moving. A river of blood flowed from the hole in his throat. The thick carpet sopped up most but not all of it.

I felt a little like Lady Macbeth. "Yet who would have thought the old man to have had so much blood in him?" But the little lady was swimming in guilt, and I couldn't feel anything but numb satisfaction no matter how hard I tried. Nobody ever deserved death more thoroughly. Nobody's death ever came in a more appropriate manner.

Just for the record I took his pulse. He turned out to be just as dead as he looked. Then I walked over to Billy, grabbed hold of his wrist, and found out he was as dead as his boss. I glanced at Ralph—he didn't seem to be breathing, and when I looked for a pulse I couldn't find one. Maybe he had a heart attack. Maybe I scared him to death.

Then I saw beads of blood in both his ears and figured out what happened. The fall with Billy on top of him had been a healthy one. He fractured his skull and he was dead.

Which meant there were three of them. Three dead men on a thick carpet in an ugly living room. Three bodies cooling off under a beamed ceiling in a Long Island manor house. Three gunshots in ten minutes.

And one worn-out detective who needed a drink. Badly.

And all at once I remembered another picture. A picture of an apartment where a dead and nearly nude blonde lay still and silent in the center of an immaculate room. The scene I was in now was just as surrealistic. Maybe it was Death itself that was surrealistic. Maybe the rest was just the frame for the picture.

I got out of there in a hurry. I wiped off everything I could have touched in one way or another—a doorknob here, a chair there. I wiped off three hands and wrists while I tried to remember whether it was possible to get a print from a dead man's skin. I took a final look at the three of them and remembered they had been alive just a few minutes ago, all three of them, and that I was responsible for their deaths.

I wasn't sorry.

I remembered the beating they had handed me and the search they had given my apartment. I thought about all the people they had managed to mess up in one way or another in the course of their lives. So I wasn't sorry at all. They had it coming.

I picked up the briefcase. It was beginning to feel like an old friend. I carried it out of the house, wiped the brass doorknob and closed the carved oak door. The bullet in Bannister's throat was my only souvenir. And ballistics wouldn't be able to do a thing with it. Peter Armin wouldn't own a traceable gun.

From the front seat of the Chevy I looked out at the house again. Bannister's house, his estate. The sun was still shining and I blinked at it. I'd been expecting dark clouds and gloomy weather. But the real world doesn't have the artistic balance of a Gothic novel. Bannister's lawn was still neat, still blindingly green. Birds went on singing in his trees.

They didn't seem to miss him at all.

I pushed the accelerator to the floor and let the Chevy have her head. The top was still down and the rush of very fresh air shook me out of my mood. A few miles down the road I pulled over to the curb to fill a pipe and get it going. There was a small hole in my right-hand jacket pocket, the one the bullet went through. It was black around the edges. The gun in that pocket felt heavier now than before. Actually it was lighter by a bullet. It still felt heavier.

I goosed the Chevy and we got going again.

There was one little headache—I'd beaten the brains out of a little guy with glasses, and unless Bannister was lying for the sheer hell of it the guy hadn't been tailing me at all. But that was something to worry about later. For the time being I had plenty to do. I had answers to all the questions now, values for all the unknowns in my human equation. X and Y and Z had names and shapes and faces. I knew all I had to know.

I left Suffolk County behind, hurried through Nassau, got done with Queens as quickly as I could. I rode under the East River, felt trapped in the tunnel, then came out in Manhattan again. It felt good. I'm a city boy—I was born here and I like it here, and it's the only spot that feels like home. Boroughs like Brooklyn and Queens are a waste of time and space, and the rest of Long Island is the country.

"And the country is a healthy grave."

There was a parking space down the block from my building. It was a tight squeeze but the Chevy fit in it. I slipped the briefcase out of sight under the front seat, walked to my door with my right arm draped over the bullethole in my pocket. In my own apartment I got out of the jacket, emptied its pockets and heaved it down the incinerator. It was a shame, because it was kind of a nice jacket, but it had to go. I put on a fresh jacket, put wallet and handkerchief and gun in the right pockets, and poured out a slug of cognac. I sat down in a chair and worked on the cognac while I flipped through the *Times* at long last.

I wasn't exactly killing time. In the first place, I needed the drink. In the second, there was a chance that the Alicia bit was still getting an occasional few lines of printer's ink, and I wanted to know about it if it was. So I sipped and flipped, in approximately that order. There was nothing about the late Alicia Arden. There was something else.

I almost missed it. It was on one of those catchall back pages, a short bit most of the way down the fifth column. I noticed it because they had happened to run a picture with it and pictures on the inside back pages are rare. This was a good news photo—a clear and infinitely sad shot of a dead little man propped up against a brick warehouse wall.

So I read the article. Nothing sensational, nothing spectacularly newsworthy. The sad little man in the photograph had been found in the very small hours of the morning after having been shot twice in the center of his chest. Police found him in the very West Thirties, the warehouse district on the wrong side of Eleventh Avenue.

He had been killed elsewhere and dumped where he was found. In addition to the bullets, he'd been beaten around the face.

There had been no identification yet. He'd had no wallet, no papers. His fingerprints were not on file. He had one identifying mark, a six-digit number tattooed on his right forearm.

Nothing much at all. But it made me look at the picture again, and it actually took a second look to recognize him. His face had never been the memorable sort and it was less so in a news photo. But I had seen him before.

He was the tail I'd pounded on Times Square the night before.

I went back to the car. The briefcase was still on the floor under the seat, right where I had left it. I put it next to me and started the engine. I had a little more trouble getting out of the space than getting in, but the Chevy was in a good mood and we made it.

It was time to deliver the briefcase and collect my reward.

THIRTEEN

THE air was gray, the sun smothered by clouds. Eighth Avenue swam with the human debris of late afternoon. A pair of well-dressed Negro pimps stood like cigar store Indians in front of the Greek movie theater across the street. A Madison Avenue type, his attaché case at his feet, leafed dispassionately and sadly through a bin of pornographic pictures in a bookstore. Taxi drivers honked their horns and pedestrians dodged rush-hour traffic. All over neon signs winked in electric seduction.

The Chevy was parked on Forty-fifth Street. I left it there and went into the Ruskin with the briefcase tucked under one arm. I found the taproom and had a double cognac. It went down smoothly and made a warm spot in my stomach.

In the lobby I picked up the house phone and called Peter Armin. He picked up the phone right off the bat.

"London," I said. "Busy?"

He wasn't.

"I've got a present for you," I told him. "Okay to bring it right up?"

A low chuckle came over the phone. "You're an amazing man, Mr. London. Come right up. I'll be anxious to see you."

I rang off, stuffed tobacco into a pipe and lit it. I walked to the elevator. The operator was a sleepy-eyed kid with a very short brushcut and a wad of gum in his mouth. He chewed it all the way to the eleventh floor, telling me at the same time who was going to win the fight at St. Nick's that night. I yeahed him along, got out of the car and found Armin's door. I knocked on it and he opened it.

131

"Mr. London," he said. "Come in. Please come in."

We went inside. He closed the door, then turned to me again. I looked at him while he looked at the briefcase I was holding. He was very pleased to see it. His clothes were different again—chocolate slacks, a dark brown silk shirt, a tan cashmere cardigan. I wondered how many changes of clothes he carried around in that suitcase of his.

"An amazing man," he said softly. "You and I make a pact. Within twenty-four hours you produce the briefcase. One might almost be tempted to presume you'd had it all along. But I'm sure that's not the truth."

"It isn't."

"May I ask how you took possession of it?"

I shrugged. "Somebody dropped it in my lap."

"Just like that?"

"Just like that."

"Amazing, truly amazing. And Mr. Bannister? Have you any news of Mr. Bannister?"

"He's dead."

"You killed him?"

"I think he had a heart attack."

He chuckled again. "Marvellous, Mr. London. De mortuis, of course. De mortuis nil nisi bonum. Yet I cannot avoid thinking that few men have merited a heart attack more whole-heartedly, if you'll excuse the play on words. You're a man of action, Mr. London, and a man of economy as well. You waste neither time nor words. A rare and enviable combination in these perilous times."

He stopped, reached into a pocket of the cardigan and dragged out his Turkish cigarettes. He offered me one, as usual. I passed it up, as usual. He took one himself and lit it.

"Now," he said. "If I might have the briefcase?"

"One thing first."

"Oh?"

"A matter of money," I said. "Something like five thousand."

He was all apologies. He scurried over to the dresser, opened the bottom drawer, drew out a small gray steel lockbox with a combination lock. He spun dials mysteriously and the box opened. There was an envelope inside it. He took it out and presented it solemnly to me.

"Five thousand," he said. "The bills are perfectly good and perfectly untraceable. If you'd like to count them——"

"I'll trust you," I said. I stuffed the envelope in my inside jacket pocket.

"Now the briefcase?"

I said: "Of course." I handed it to him and he took it from me, his small hands trembling slightly. He accepted the case the way a man takes into his arms a woman he has lusted after without success for a long period of time. I stood and watched him as he sat down in his chair and opened it.

He reacted just the way he was supposed to. He unzipped the briefcase quickly, ignored the letter and opened the pouch with the keys in it. He took them out, looked them over.

His face changed expression.

For a moment or two he sat still as Death and did not say a word. Then, his eyes still on the keys, he said: "There seems to be some sort of mistake, Mr. London."

I didn't say anything.

"Something's gone wrong," he said. "Somewhere along the line there's been a slip. These are not the right keys."

"Of course not," I said. "I know that, Mr. Wallstein."

The words sank in slowly. He stayed where he was, not moving at all for a minute or two. Then his eyes left the keys and climbed an inch at a time until they were looking at me.

They widened when they were focussed on the Beretta in my hand.

He said nothing at first. His face changed expression several times and I could see his mind working, looking for avenues of escape, seeing each in turn sealed off in front of him. When he got around to speaking his voice was a thousand years old. He sounded like a man who had been running very hard and very fast for a very long time. And who was now discovering that he had been running in the wrong direction.

133

"A most amazing man," he said. "And just how much do you know, Mr. London?"

"Most of it."

He sighed. "Tell me," he said. "I'd like to see how much you know and how you determined it. I don't suppose it will be much in the way of consolation. But it's important for a man to know just where he cut his own throat."

"Keep your hands where I can see them."

"Certainly," he said. He placed them palms-down on his knees. "And if you could point that gun elsewhere—"

He had shown me the same courtesy before, in my own apartment. I could hardly refuse him. I lowered the gun slightly.

I said: "Your name is Franz Wallstein. You occupied a fairly important position in Nazi Germany. You stole a small fortune in jewels and managed to make a clean break when the roof fell in in 1945. You ran for Mexico, then skipped to Buenos Aires. You set yourself up as an importer under the name Heinz Linder and you were doing pretty well. Then the Israelis found your trail again."

"They are relentless," he said.

"But you had advance warning. Not much warning—it didn't leave you time to cash in your home or your business. But you did have enough time to make sure your trail would end forever in Buenos Aires. You found some one who looked enough like you to pass for you. He didn't have to be a perfect double—you'd been under wraps for fifteen years. You took him home with you and shot him dead."

He listened with no trace of expression on his face. I got the impression that he was discovering himself now in the words I spoke. His eyes were deep, his features relaxed.

"Maybe you bought cooperation from the government," I went on. "That's supposed to be pretty easy in Argentina. At any rate, you left your double dead in your home and let the Israelis take credit for the kill. Then you staged a robbery—filled your suitcase with jewels and caught the first plane to Canada. It was an easier

134

country to enter than the United States. But it wasn't as easy to set up shop there as it was in Argentina. You've got expensive tastes. The money must have gone pretty quickly. You needed more money and you needed it in a hurry."

"Debts pile up," he said softly. "And a hunted man must keep his credit good." There was the ghost of a smile on his lips.

"You still had the jewels. They were negotiable, especially if you sold them off a few at a time. But that wasn't good enough for you. You wanted to latch onto the money without letting go of the jewels. You're a man who likes beautiful things and you wanted to keep them."

I paused. "Am I right so far?"

"More or less. I could never have received a shadow of their worth. And they're very beautiful stones, Mr. London."

"They must be. Let's take it a little further. You met Alicia Arden. She knew about a fence—Bannister. That was fine, but you still wanted to sell the jewels without letting go. So the two of you cooked up a swindle. You managed to hook up with three or four professional thieves and you sold them on the notion of acting as agents for the sale of the jewels. According to what you told them, they would go to New York to handle the transfer of the gems for the money."

"It's common enough," he said. "They took their chances in return for a cut of the proceeds."

"That was the setup, sure. You even let them cache the jewels and make up only one set of keys. That was to keep you from stealing the stuff back and leaving Bannister holding the briefcase. They were honest thieves, as you said. But they weren't careful enough. You and Alicia fixed things so that both Bannister and the thieves would be out in the cold."

"You know the details, Mr. London?"

I looked at him. I wondered where Maddy was, what she was doing. I glanced out the window and watched the sky turn darker. I looked back at him.

"I can guess," I said. "Alicia was supposed to come to New York to negotiate with Bannister. Then she told

Bannister he could pull a switch and save himself a hundred grand—this kept him from haggling over the price. When the time came, he gave her the money and sent her where the thieves were staying. She was supposed to trade the money for the briefcase, but instead of turning the case over to Bannister she held onto it.

"Then you came into the picture. You would get the money from the thieves and leave them for Bannister, who would get rid of them by killing them. It was neat—the thieves wouldn't be looking for you because they'd be dead. And Bannister didn't even know you were alive. You and Alicia would have the money and the jewels. Free and clear."

I drew a breath. "But she didn't play it that way, did she?"

"No," he said quietly. "She did not."

"She must have made a fresh switch of her own. She set up the deal without telling you about it."

He managed a smile. "She was supposed to make the switch on a Wednesday. It took place a day early. I did not know about it until it was over."

"She made the switch," I said. "She turned over the money to the thieves and took the briefcase in exchange. Then she called Bannister and told him they wouldn't play ball. He killed them and took his dough back. She lost the money that way—but she had the jewels all to herself now. And they were worth a hell of a lot more than a hundred grand."

He nodded, agreeing.

"So you found out about the cross. And you went hunting for Alicia Arden. You knew her very well. You knew what to look for and where to look. You didn't have Bannister's organization but you had something more valuable in your knowledge. He never found her. You did."

My pipe had been out for a while. I put it in a pocket. "So you broke in on her and killed her," I went on. "You didn't use a Beretta then. You had another gun and you used it to put a hole in her face. You killed her before you did anything else. She had crossed you and you were furious. Bannister was after her more as a matter of profit-and-loss than anything else. He might have killed her, but not unless he found the briefcase first. But you wanted her dead. That was more important than the briefcase."

His face darkened. "For each man kills the thing he loves," he quoted. "I was in love with her, Mr. London. A human fault. A reasonable man is a man who never loves. Reason goes only so far. I loved her. When she betrayed that love I killed her. Another common pattern."

He took out another cigarette and lit it. I watched him smoke. I wondered what he was thinking now.

I said: "You had to be the killer. If Bannister had killed her he would have turned the place upside-down. But you're a neat man. You wouldn't confuse a search with a sacking. You must have cleaned as you searched."

"It was easier that way."

"And you left her there," I said. "You couldn't find the briefcase so you kept the apartment under as close surveillance as you could. There was a limit—you were alone, and you couldn't be there all the time. You didn't see my friend visit the apartment. But you saw me and thought I took the briefcase."

He shook his head. "I thought you had it all along. I thought you were working with her."

"Same thing." I shrugged. "That's what I got so far. Also that you were the one who took a potshot at me when I was heading up the stairs to my apartment. Just a warning, I guess. So I'd be in a mood to team up with you."

"I wasn't trying to kill you."

"Of course not. When you really tried to kill someone, you didn't miss. I was a sitting duck there, wasn't I? But that was just a warning. Last night you didn't miss."

"Last night?"

"I know about it," I said. "I ran into the guy outside. He was in the lobby and he followed us when we left here. Maybe he thought I was a buddy of yours. Maybe he wanted to talk to me. I'll never know."

He shrugged.

"He was an old friend of yours," I went on. "I never got to know his name. Did you know it?"

"No."

"Just a little man with a harmless face. One of the little men who spent some time in that camp of yours across the ocean. A concentration camp victim looking for you. He found you, too. How long was he on your trail?"

"He wasn't."

"No?"

"He lived in New York, Mr. London. And he saw me, here in New York. And recognized me."

"And got killed for it."

"He'd have killed me, Mr. London." His shoulders heaved in another shrug. "He was willing to risk death. He cared only for revenge."

"And he got his revenge. I might have had trouble making the final connection without him. But the forearm tattoo gave it away. You had to be Wallstein then. Everything fit into place."

"You were lucky."

"I know that," I said. "Well, that's what I got. Did I come close?"

His lips curled into a smile. His chuckle sounded happy. "Too close," he said. "Far too close. There are points here and there where you're wrong. But they are really immaterial, Mr. London. They do not matter." He heaved a sigh. "I never thought you would guess this much. How did you figure it out?"

I watched him put out his cigarette. He didn't seem nervous at all. He was more interested in seeing where he missed the boat than in finding a way out. There was no reason not to tell him. It wouldn't do him any good to know.

"A magician would say you made too much use of misdirection," I told him. "An actress friend of mine would say you over-acted. From the start I had to figure out where you belonged in the overall scheme of things. Your routine about making a living by being in the right place at the right time was a little far-fetched. You knew too much. You had to belong somewhere in the middle of things. At first I guessed you were one of the thieves."

"That's what I wished you to think."

I nodded. "But you sold that too hard. You made a point of telling me what Wallstein was like, being careful to describe someone wholly unlike yourself. You made him tall and blond, a typical SS type, while you yourself are short and dark. You pictured him as a thoroughly unattractive character, one of whom you disapproved highly. Franz Wallstein, obviously, was not the kind of man you like."

A slight smile. "And perhaps that was not wholly untrue."

"Maybe not. But I wondered how you would know so much about Wallstein, even if you were one of the thieves. It seemed unlikely. And it was just as funny for you to waste so much time telling me about him. I had to guess you were selling me a bill of goods."

"Was that all?"

I shook my head. "There was more. You gave me a lot of surface detail on the profession of larceny. But you never got around to describing the very brilliant crime in which the jewels were stolen. From that I guessed that there hadn't been any crime. You were Wallstein and you stole your own jewels."

He was nodding, digesting all of it. "More," I said. "I tied you to Alicia Arden from the start. Not from what you said about her—you were properly vague. But you always called her Alicia, never used anything but the first name. I was Mr. London to you every time. Bannister was Mr. Bannister. Once I realized you weren't one of the thieves, the rest came easily."

He looked away. "I didn't even realize it," he said. "I guess she was always Alicia to me and nothing else. Of course."

He looked up at me again, his jaw set, his eyes steady. "I could offer you a great deal of money," he said. "But you have the keys as it stands. You can get the jewels without my help. Besides, I suspect a bribe would have no effect on you."

I told him it wouldn't.

He sighed. "What next, Mr. London? Where do we proceed from here?"

"That's up to you," I said.

139

"May I smoke, Mr. London?"

I told him to go ahead. I raised the gun to cover him but he didn't make any false movements. He shook out a cigarette, put it to his lips, set the end on fire with his lighter. The cigarette didn't flare up and blind me. The lighter wasn't a cleverly camouflaged gun. He lit his cigarette and he smoked it.

I lowered the gun.

"If you turn me in," he said, "you'll be faced with problems."

"I know."

"The police will want to know about your part. You broke a law or two yourself. You moved a body. You were an accessory after the fact of murder."

"I know."

"Withholding information—another crime. Not to mention Mr. Bannister's heart attack."

"That was self-defense."

"You might have difficulty proving that to the police. They might call it murder. You might go to jail."

I shrugged. "Not if I handed you to them," I said. "I think they'd make allowances."

He pursed his lips. "Perhaps," he said. "You're licensed as a private detective, aren't you? Couldn't they revoke your license?"

"If they wanted to."

"So much trouble," he said. "And they probably wouldn't even hang me. They might, but I doubt it. It would be hard to prove murder, harder still to prove premeditation. I might get life imprisonment. But not death."

"You quoted 'The Ballad of Reading Gaol' a while back," I reminded him. "Know the rest of it?"

He nodded. "I'm fond of Oscar Wilde."

"Then you remember his description of prison. And of course you had something to do with a prison yourself, didn't you?"

"Our prisons were worse, Mr. London. Much worse. The Austrian corporal had unhappy ideas. American prisons are not like that."

"They're no bed of roses," I said. "And if they do electrocute you, it won't be nice. It's worse than being mur-

140

dered. All the anticipation before hand. It's not nice."

We sat and looked at each other for minute or two. The verbal fencing wasn't a hell of a lot of fun. I wanted to be out of there, to get away from him.

"So the situation is unhappy for us both," he said. "Wouldn't it be simpler to let me go free?"

"It would."

"But you won't?"

"No," I said. "I won't."

"Because of what I am? Because I'm Franz Wallstein?"

"Because you killed the girl."

A long sigh. "You would have to be a moral man, Mr. London. It's unfortunate."

I shook my head. I said: "It's not a matter of morality. It's tough enough living with myself the way things stand. It would be tougher if I let you go. I'm practical, not moral."

"And you find it more practical to turn me in than to let me go?"

"Yes."

"No matter how much trouble it causes you?"

"Yes."

We killed a few more seconds. The sky was almost black now. In a few minutes it was going to start raining. I wondered how Maddy's audition went. I wondered where she was and what she was doing. I wanted to be with her.

"Mr. London—"

I waited.

"I've said this before in quite another context. We are both reasonable men."

"To a point."

"Of course, to a point. But there is a way for you to achieve your objective without trouble. It would simplify your problems and mine as well. It would be easier for us both."

I nodded.

"Do you know what I mean?"

"I think so."

"Justice will be served," he said. "Whatever precisely justice may be. Expedience, quite another goddess, will

141

be served as well. And I think you shall find it no more difficult to live with yourself as a result. Do you follow me?"

"Yes," I said. "I follow you."

He got to his feet. "Now follow me literally," he said. "Keep your gun on me. Because I'll kill you if given the chance. You shouldn't give me that chance."

I didn't. I stayed behind him and I kept the Beretta centered on his back. He led the way to the bathroom, opened the door of the medicine cabinet. He took out a small phial of pills, held it up and studied the contents thoughtfully.

"I've carried them for so long a time," he said. "When the Reich fell we all supplied ourselves with them. I've had them ever since. Some of us carried them in our mouths, ready to bite down on the capsule when it became necessary. Himmler managed that. He cheated his captors, died before their eyes."

I didn't say anything.

"I've had them with me ever since," he went on. "Even when I felt most secure they were always within reach. Habit, perhaps. I almost took them once. It was in Mexico City. I was in the air terminal waiting for a plane and two Jewish agents passed within arm's reach of me. I had a pill in my mouth. I was ready to use it the minute I was recognized. But they did not recognize me."

He uncapped the phial and tilted it. A large brown capsule rolled into the palm of his hand. He studied it.

"I threw that pill away," he said. "Not then. Not until I was in Buenoes Aires. I took it from my mouth when I stepped onto the plane, and I sat in my seat in the plane with the pill clutched in my hand. I expected agents to meet the plane. They did not. I took an apartment in Buenoes Aires and threw the pill away. But I kept the others. And now I have occasion to use them."

There was a glass on the shelf over the sink. It was still in its cellophane wrapper. He set the pill on the shelf and unwrapped the glass. He let the water run for a minute or two, then filled the glass to the brim.

"I'm not sure about this," he said. "Do I swallow the pill or crush it in my teeth? Swallowing would be simplier. But the capsule might not dissolve. It didn't dissolve when I had it in my mouth."

He went on talking in the same gentle tone of voice. "I could have thrown the water in your face," he said. "It would have been a chance, if a slim one. But I think you would have shot me. And the shot might not have killed me, and then we would have had the unpleasantness of police and a trial and the rest. It's really not worth the chance. But how do you measure worth here? Is it worth any risk to save one's life? All the logic in the world won't answer that question."

He poured the water into the sink, put the glass back on the shelf. He picked up the pill and held it between thumb and forefinger.

"They're supposed to be painless," he said. "Almost instantaneous. I wonder if that's so or not. I really hope so. I'm a physical coward, Mr. London."

"You're a brave man."

"That's not true," he said. "Bravery and resignation are not synonymous, not by any means. I'm simply a resigned coward."

He put the pill in his mouth. Then he changed his mind and took it out again.

"There's one point," he said. "You might as well know this. I lied to you about one thing. I did it more to simplify procedures than anything else. Alicia wasn't nude when I left her. After I killed her, that is."

"I know."

"Do you know what she was wearing?"

"Yes."

A smile. "You know so many things, Mr. London. There are things I wish I knew. I wish I knew just what will happen after I put this little pill to use. Will it end there? The religious myths are really a little hard to take, yet I wish I could accept them. Even Hell would be preferable to simple nonexistence. The churches make a mistake, you know. Simple nothingness is more terrible than any Hell they have managed to devise. Sulphur and brimstone cannot compare."

"Maybe it's like going to sleep."

He shook his head. "Sleep implies an eventual awak-

143

ening. But I'm afraid it's a moot point. A semantic game. And why puzzle over it when I can find out the answer in an instant?"

I wanted to tell him to put down the pill, to run, to catch a plane and disappear. But I thought of the dead blonde and the dead thieves and the corpse in Argentina. I thought of a little man found leaning against a Hell's Kitchen warehouse, and I thought of six million of his relatives in German ovens.

I still wanted to let him go.

He smiled at me. Then he popped the pill into his mouth and closed his eyes. His jaws twitched once as he bit into the pill. His eyes opened, and for a tiny speck of time he looked at me. Then he fell to the floor and died.

FOURTEEN

I GAVE my car back to the garage. The same kid was still on duty and he had something suitably inane to say. But I didn't hear it. I wasn't listening.

The air smelled of a storm on the way. It had begun that way and it was ending the same way, with the city crouching under rain clouds. I walked home with the briefcase under my arm. I climbed the stairs and nobody shot at me from behind. I unlocked my door and went inside. There were no surprises—no dark little men with guns, no briefcases, no disorder. Just my apartment, just as I had left it.

I filled a glass with cognac and worked on it. I thought about love and death. I thought about Alicia Arden, about the kind of girl she must have been, about the girl she had been to the men who had known her. I thought about a girl of my own and found myself smiling. I picked up the phone and dialed Maddy's number.

"Hi," I said. "How was the audition?"

"Ed," she chirped. "Oh, it was fine, it was great, I'll tell you about it later. But what happened? Are you all right?"

"I'm fine."

"How . . . how did everything go?"

"All right. Lots of things happened."

"Tell me. You didn't get hurt, did you? You're all right?"

"I'm fine," I said again. "I'll tell you when I see you."

"Can you come right down? Or should I come up?"

"Neither," I said. "I'll be down in an hour or so. We can grab a late dinner. I'll take you out and feed you."

"I'll cook, Ed. I feel like cooking tonight. Why don't

145

you come down right away? I thought you were all finished."

"Almost," I said. "I'll see you in two hours at the outside. And cook a big dinner. I'll need it."

I stood there a moment, thought about her, remembered how her voice sounded. I wondered what was coming up next for us, what she would be to me and what I would be to her. I thought about love, about its effect on some people I knew. It was either the most essential single thing in the world or the one thing a man had to learn to get by without, and I couldn't make up my mind which way it worked. You could argue either side.

I lit a pipe, poured more cognac. And made another phone call.

Kaye answered. When she recognized my voice she started talking very fast and very shakily.

"Oh, Ed," she said. "Ed, I've been worrying about you. What's the matter?"

"Nothing's the matter," I told her. "What do you mean?"

She hesitated. "Oh, I don't know. But you've been calling Jack and seeing Jack and I was all worried."

"What about?"

"About you."

"Me?"

A pause. "Ed, if you're . . . sick . . . you can tell me, Ed. I have a right to know. I——"

I laughed, as much out of relief as anything else. "It's not for me," I improvised. "It's for Jack. He needed a detective and wanted to keep the business in the family. A few clients did a skip and he wanted me to run a tracer on them, get them to pay their bills. I don't think you should worry yourself sick over it."

She sounded very happy. "But I worry," she said. "I mean, you're all alone in the world, Ed."

"I've got a pretty sweet sister——"

"You know what I mean. If you had a wife to take care of you I wouldn't worry."

I laughed again. "Maybe I will," I said. "Soon."

"You've got a girl?"

"Dozens of them. But there's one who's been getting

146

important. I'll tell you all about it one of these days. Look, put your husband on, will you?"

She said something sweet, and I said something sweet, and then she put her husband on.

And I talked to him.

After that I took a fast shower and a faster shave. The shave was a little too fast—I wound up slicing off part of my face. I couldn't stop the bleeding with a styptic pencil so I slapped a Band-Aid on the gash and grinned at myself in the mirror. Just everybody in New York had swung at me or shoved a gun in my face in the past few days, and the only way I could get hurt was by cutting myself with my own razor. Hell, maybe it would leave an interesting scar.

I went back to the living room. Then I sat down in one of the leather chairs and waited for him.

He knocked at the door. When I told him it was open he came in, a little out of breath, his hair poorly combed and his face redder than usual. His tie was loose and his face was weak with the same fear I'd seen there before.

"I got here as soon as I could," he said. "Hope I didn't keep you waiting, Ed. Something the matter?"

I took a step toward him. I threw the briefcase at him and he raised his hands instinctively to block it. It bounced off his hands and landed on the floor.

"This is yours," I said. "You forgot it last time you were here."

"For God's sake, Ed!"

"You son of a bitch," I said. "You rotten bastard."

I hit him in the face. He backed off, his hands up to cover his face, and I belted him in the middle. When he folded up I hit him in the face and he went to the floor. He started to get up.

I said: "Stay there, Jack. If you get up I'll knock the crap out of you."

He stayed there.

"I never suspected you," I told him. "Never. Hell, I didn't want to suspect you. You were Kaye's husband, I was doing you a favor to begin with. And you played me

147

for a sucker from the word go. You're a rotten son of a bitch, Jack."

He opened his mouth. I waited for him to say something but he changed his mind. He bit his lip, closed his mouth. He looked away from me.

"How did you meet Alicia?"

"I told you. She came to my office."

"Was that part true?"

He nodded.

"Then that's where the truth stopped. You met her and the two of you wound up in the hay. You were mannered and polished and socially acceptable and she was warm and blonde and good in bed. So the two of you hit it off fine.

"She was also talkative. She told you all about Wallstein and Bannister and a half-million bucks worth of stolen jewels."

"Ed——"

"Shut up. This didn't happen on East Fifty-first Street. It happened in her apartment in the Village. Because the apartment and the alias came later. She never thought of them. They were your ideas. The whole double-cross gimmick was your idea all the way, wasn't it?"

"It just happened," he said.

"Happened?"

"You know what I mean. We were talking about . . . the jewels. And we both thought——"

"I think it was your idea, Jack."

He didn't say anything.

I said: "She was a floater all the way, took things as they came. Her life wasn't easy but she knew how to get by. She was Wallstein's mistress and he idolized her. And he was going to have enough money to keep her happy as soon as his deal went through. No, I don't think she could have thought of the double cross. That had to be your idea."

I looked at him and saw how weak and gutless he was. I was hoping he would get up so I could knock him down again. I remembered Wallstein telling me I wasn't a violent man. But now I felt violent.

"So you rented an apartment for her," I went on.

"And gave her a phony name. And just to be safe you took the briefcase away from her. Why? Didn't you trust her?"

"Of course I did. Damn it, I loved her!"

"Then why did you take the briefcase? Why not let her hold onto it? Because you had the case all along, Jack. That's why Wallstein didn't find it when he killed her. It wasn't there. Why take it if you trusted her?"

"I thought it would be safer with me."

"Safer from whom?"

"Wallstein, Bannister. Everybody."

"Then you didn't think she was very safe, did you?" He looked up, puzzled. "Even with the new apartment and the alias, you knew somebody might get to her. And if they did, you wanted to make sure you had the briefcase. She wasn't so important. But the jewels were."

"That's a lie!"

"Is it?"

He looked at the floor again. "She was all that mattered," he said brokenly. "I didn't care about the jewels. I didn't give a damn about them. I was in love with her."

I let it go. "You had it all set up with her," I said. "You doped out a way to cross Wallstein and Bannister both at once. Then you and Alicia would lie low for a while. I suppose after that you were going to skip the country. Where were you going to go?"

"Brazil. I don't know."

"And live happily ever after. But Wallstein got to her first. He loved her, too—everybody loved that girl, Jack. He loved her enough to kill her after she crossed him up. And Wallstein wasn't the sort of man who killed if he could avoid it."

"He was a crook." His eyes flared. "He was a rotten Nazi."

"He was also a better man than you are. He killed her and he went through that apartment from floor to ceiling looking for a briefcase that wasn't there. Because you had it.

"She was already dead when you got there. And you fell apart, Jack. Suddenly the whole world was falling in on you. Hell, you were scared green. That's when you stripped her."

His mouth fell open.

"Yeah, you stripped her. That's the only way it adds up. She was wearing something that could be traced to you. Or you thought it could. I can even guess what it was. You told me once how she liked to sit around the house in that man's bathrobe you bought her. Was that what she was wearing?"

He nodded slowly.

"Maybe the stockings and garter belt were underneath the robe. Maybe she was nude and you started to dress her, got as far as the belt and the stockings and panicked. It doesn't make a hell of a lot of difference. Either way, this girl you loved so much was dead as a lox and you were busy staying in the clear. You were noble as hell, Jack."

He closed his eyes. "I couldn't think straight," he mumbled. "I didn't know what I was doing."

"That's an understatement. You were blundering around like a kid in a cathouse. By the time you got out of there you realized that you could burn all the bathrobes in the world without getting clear. You had to get the body out of that apartment or it would be traced to you. But you didn't have the guts to do your own dirty work. You came running to me with a scrambled story, confessed to cheating on Kaye in order to cover up all the rest of it. And you fooled me, damn it. I moved the girl's body and got you out of it."

I lit my pipe. "Remember what you told me a few minutes ago? The briefcase wasn't important to you. The girl was all that mattered. You said so, right?"

He nodded.

"And you lied. You had that briefcase and you weren't going to give it up no matter how dead Alicia was. You never thought of telling me about it."

"I didn't want to . . . complicate things."

"You didn't want to pass up a fortune. That's more like it. By the time I moved the body you were making a deal of your own with Bannister. You called him up, ready to sell him the briefcase and make a quick profit

150

for yourself. With Alicia dead there wasn't any point to running for Brazil. But you could still use a hundred grand tax free. You called Bannister and tried to work a deal. He wanted to know who you were. And you got scared.

"I thought he would kill me."

"So you threw him a bone," I said. "You gave him my name."

"I wasn't thinking."

"That's a good excuse, isn't it? You use it every other sentence. It's a little worn out now. Anyway, Bannister wasn't as stupid as you were. The minute he had me on the phone he knew I wasn't the guy who called him in the first place. But you gave him a place to start. I was the only name he knew and he decided to work me over for all I was worth. He put a pair of thugs on my neck and they gave me a hard time. And that was your fault."

"I didn't know——"

"You never knew anything." I was disgusted with him. "You loused up everything you touched. You were the clumsiest clod in history. Your lies were so clumsy I believed them and your actions were so stupid they were impossible to analyze. First you were going to skip the country with Alicia and the jewels. Then she was dead and you were set to sell the jewels on your own. Finally things got so shaky you were scared to breathe. The money didn't look so big any more. My phone call this morning had you jumping out of your skin, didn't it?"

"Yes. I was afraid."

I nodded. "So you wanted to get rid of the briefcase. It was simple once you found out I wasn't home. While I waited for your call, you came over here. Maybe you were going to stick the briefcase under my mat, then found the key and came inside. You dropped the case on the coffee table and called me from my own phone. That was a cute touch. So you must have figured you were lucky to be out of it. You still had Kaye and the kids, even if you didn't care about them——"

"I——"

"Don't tell me how much you love them," I said. "I'm sick of all your passionate attachments. You had your

151

wife and your daughters and your position and your practice. The romantic life just wasn't worth it any more; you were happy to be in the clear. That's why you were so glad to switch that line of yours about how Alicia and the apartment looked when you found her. Anything to let yourself off the hook."

He was silent now. I turned my back on him and poured a drink, half-hoping he'd make a break for it so I could have an excuse to take him apart again. But hitting him wouldn't be much of a kick now. The hatred and anger were slipping away and contempt was taking their place. He wasn't worth hitting.

"Get up," I said.

He looked worried. "Go on," I said. "Get up. I'm not going to hit you. I'm sick of looking at you—you look pretty damned silly on the floor."

He stood up shakily. His eyes were wary.

"Jack, why?"

I watched him while he thought about it. He took his time getting his answers ready, and when he got going I had the feeling that he was talking as much to himself as to me.

"I'm not sure," he said. "I . . . Kaye and I haven't loved each other in years. A marriage can get very stale without going completely dead. We went stale."

"Just like that?"

"A little at a time. I don't know. I sat around in a rut and didn't know it. Maybe I made a mistake going into medicine. I was never that crazy to be a doctor. Money and respect and security—they motivated me more than any real interest in medicine. And then I met Alicia."

He paused for breath. "Each of us was just right for the other, Ed. It was almost chemical. A chemical reaction. She was a footloose thing who never knew what was going to happen next to her. She'd been a prostitute and a marijuana smoker and a con-man's partner and everything else under the sun. She told me stories that made my hair curl. She was excitement for me; I wasn't in a rut any more."

"Go on."

152

"I don't know. I had to make one big break, one stab in the right direction. With the money from the jewels we could make a whole new life for ourselves. It looked too good to be true."

"How long before the new life turned into a rut?"

"It wouldn't have happened," he said doggedly.

"Sure."

"Ed, we loved each other."

"Sure. You loved Kaye once, didn't you?"

He sighed. "That was different. I was a different man, a younger man. It was a different sort of love. I loved Alicia very much."

"So you killed her."

He stared at me. He started to say something but I didn't give him a chance. I held up a hand to shut him up.

I said: "You killed her. You and Wallstein both loved her and both of you killed her. You set her up for him. If you weren't in the picture, she and Wallstein would have pulled off their swindle. They'd have wound up safe in Canada. You made her cross him and he killed her. He was a braver man than you, Jack. He killed her with a sword. You killed her with a kiss."

After a very long moment he gave me a slow nod. I waited for him to say something.

"You ought to kill me," he said finally.

"Probably."

"You should."

I shook my head. "I've killed too many men today," I told him. "Four of them. Can you believe it? Four men, and you're worse than any of them. But I'm sick of killing and sicker of playing God. I couldn't kill you."

"What . . . what are you going to do with me?"

"I can't turn you over to the cops," I said. "And it would be silly as hell even if I could. I'd be hurting Kaye and the girls more than you. And I can't even beat you up—I haven't got the stomach for it. You're a rotten son of a bitch and I can't do a thing to you."

He stood there and didn't say a word.

I said: "Get out of here. Get out, get away from me, stay away from me. I don't want to see you again or speak to you again. Go home to Kaye and pretend you're a husband. She needs you. I don't know how in hell anybody could need somebody like you, but she needs you. She can have you."

He didn't move.

"Damn you, get out!"

He turned and walked to the door. He opened it and left, closed it behind him. I heard him go down the stairs and leave the building.

I went over to the window. It was raining now, big heavy drops that soaked the pavement. I opened the window to let some fresh air into the place.

FIFTEEN

SHE sat across from me with one elbow on the table and her forehead resting in the palm of her hand. With her other hand she held a spoon and stirred a cup of black coffee. Her eyes were focussed on the coffee. She wore a pale green sweater over a simple white blouse and she looked beautiful.

I wondered what it would be like to sit across a table from her two or three times a day. I could think of worse ways to spend a day. Or a week, or a lifetime.

She said: "Curiouser and curiouser, said Alice."

"You don't get it?"

She shook her head. "No, that's not it. I understand what happened and everything. But the people are confusing."

"I know."

"That Peter Armin. I suppose I should call him Wallstein, shouldn't I? But I can't think of him that way. He ... didn't seem like a Nazi. I just can't picture him sticking out his hand and screaming 'Heil Hitler.' It's not consistent."

"He wasn't exactly a storm trooper, Maddy."

"Hardly. He was more like . . . oh, who was the one? The propaganda one. You know who I mean."

"Goebbels," I said. "Joseph Goebbels, Minister of Propaganda. Hitler's brain. I think you're right. Wallstein was that kind of guy."

She screwed up her face. "I liked Armin, Ed. Isn't that silly? I actually liked the man."

"I liked him myself."

"And Enright turned out to be such a bastard. And he doesn't get punished."

155

"You're wrong."

"I am?"

I nodded. "There's a balance here. It's pretty neat. Death was the worst punishment for Bannister and his boys. And for Wallstein. And life is the worst punishment for Jack Enright."

She sat back and thought it over. "Uh-huh," she said finally. "Yes, I suppose you're right. I see what you mean."

She got up to get the pot and pour us each another cup of coffee. I took a sip. It was a little too hot and I set it down to cool. I liked the way she made coffee. I liked the way she cooked.

"She must have been quite a girl," she said suddenly.

"Alicia?"

"Uh-huh. Or Sheila. Everybody has two names. Did you notice that? It makes it hard to talk straight. Oh, you know what I mean. She must have been . . . interesting."

"Because of what she did?"

"Not that so much. Because of the effect she had on men. Wallstein and Enright both fell in love with her. And the two of them were so completely different."

"Maybe they each saw a different girl."

"Maybe."

I tried the coffee again. "They were different men," I said. "That's what had me spinning around all the time. Wallstein was a pro and Enright was a total amateur. Each of them acted differently and lied differently. As soon as I caught onto that much everything got a hell of a lot simpler.

"Wallstein used misdirection. He was a pro and he lied like a pro. Enright didn't know how to lie. Hell, he couldn't tell me a thing about Alicia without tipping his hand. In his place Wallstein would have invented a whole background for the gal to throw me off the trail. All Jack did was play it dumb and tell me he didn't know anything about her."

"He said she was in the theater——"

"Uh-huh. He picked that one out of the air. She must have mentioned the party she went to with Bannister back when she was setting up the deal. He tossed me that one to make me happy, handed it to me for the hell of it."

She was nodding. "And the same goes for the apartment and everything about it."

"Right. He had his way of lying and so did Wallstein. They must have had separate ways to love her. And to kill her."

I took her hand and rubbed my fingers across the back of it. I looked down at the top of her head. Her hair was clean and fresh. I listened to the rain outside, smelled fresh coffee, thought about things.

"Ed? I just thought of something. The police will investigate, won't they?"

"Hell, they ought to. They'll find three corpses in Avalon and a fourth in the Ruskin. If they don't investigate they've got rocks in their heads."

"Won't they tie you in?"

"Not a chance," I said. "Wallstein will go as an obvious suicide. They won't even dust for prints and they won't turn mine up even if they do. I left his Beretta there—if they run a ballistics check on it they can award him posthumously with Bannister's murder, call it triple murder and suicide. It's nutty that way but it closes their file for them."

She nodded. "How about the money?"

I looked at her.

"The five thousand dollars you took from Armin."

"I'm keeping it."

"But——"

"Hell," I said, "there's nothing else to do with it. He doesn't have any heirs. And I can use five grand, Maddy. I've got as much right to it as anybody else."

She thought it over. "You're right," she said. "I guess. What about the jewels."

"Those I don't keep. I can rationalize five thousand bucks but not half a million. And I wouldn't know what to do with that kind of money. One way or another it would make a slave out of me."

"So what do you do with them?"

"I already did it," I said. "I put the right keys in an

157

envelope along with an anonymous covering letter with all the details. I sent them to the Israeli embassy. Hell, the original owners are probably dead. And they'd probably have wanted the jewels to go to Israel. They've got more right to them than anybody else I can think of."

"I see."

"Oh, to hell with it," I said. "It's just a way to get rid of them, to tell you the truth. I don't care what they do with those jewels. They can irrigate the goddam Negev or buy guns to shoot poor barefoot Arabs with. I don't give a damn what happens to the jewels. Just so I'm rid of them."

She didn't answer. We drifted off into one of those long silences that come over you when you run out of the subject of a conversation. I looked at her and tried to figure out whether she agreed with the decisions I had made, and then I started wondering why in hell I should care what she thought about it.

I thought that maybe I loved her—whatever that meant—and I thought about two other men in love and what love had done to them, what it had made them do.

It was still raining outside. I had taken a cab to her apartment, leaving the Chevy in the garage, and I knew what was going to happen next. The two of us would manage to decide that it was raining pitchforks out there, by God, that I'd have a hell of a time catching a cab, that I might as well stay the night. And we would sit quietly together and listen to quiet music, both of us trying to be properly nonchalant until it was a decent time to crawl into bed.

I knew this was going to happen and I wasn't ready to complain about it. What I didn't know was what was going to happen next. In another day or another week or another month.

I broke the silence. "The audition," I said. "You were going to tell me."

She clapped her hands like a happy child. "Oh, God! I forgot completely. Your news upstaged mine. Ed, I read that part and he loved me. He positively loved me."

"You got the part?"

"He wants me to read again, or at least he said so.

But while I was waiting for you I got a call from Maury and he said it's in the bag. Kaspar thought I was the greatest thing since vaudeville and I couldn't miss. The reading's some kind of formality."

I told her it sounded great.

"More than great," she said. "It's marvellous and magnificent and delerious and delovely and everything." Her face went serious again. "This could be that break we were talking about, Ed. Kaspar has a hell of a reputation and the play is beautiful. Really beautiful. And the critics will eat it up. They always go nuts over Lorca revivals—there was one a year and a half ago, just a short run, and I saw it and it was the most amateurish mess with a terrible cast and rotten direction. And they got rave reviews."

She paused and breathed again. "It could be a tremendous break," she said.

"When do you go into rehearsal?"

"Maury wasn't sure. Kaspar didn't say a word on the subject, of course. He never says anything. But Maury said Kaspar was talking about rehearsing upstate and opening out of town first. He's done that before. We'll probably leave New York around the middle of the month and spend the summer in some hole upstate, then open in New Haven or Boston at the start of the season. That's a guess, anyhow."

She smiled at me. "Will you miss me, Ed?"

"Sure," I said.

"Will you?"

"Uh-huh. Especially at night."

And then, while we talked about other things, all in preparation for the inevitable trip to the bedroom which we both wanted and needed very much, I thought about some other things that had been going through my mind. Thoughts about how she looked in the morning, how she would be to come home to. How the name Maddy London sounded.

That kind of thing.

Those thoughts seemed sort of silly now. Adolescent. In a week or two she'd be clearing out of town for a few months. She'd go without a thought, and by that time

159

I'd watch her go without a thought myself. Maybe something would happen with us when she came back in the fall.

And maybe not.

We carried our cups of coffee into the living room. She put soft music on the record player and we sat on the couch and listened to it. I had a little brandy. She relaxed against the arm I put around her.

"Nice place," I said.

"You like it here?"

"Uh-huh. It's easy to unwind here."

She smiled softly, and when she spoke there was a little extra emotion behind the words. "You should like it," she said. "After all, you've been here before."